Bradbury Inn

By:

K. J. Dahlen

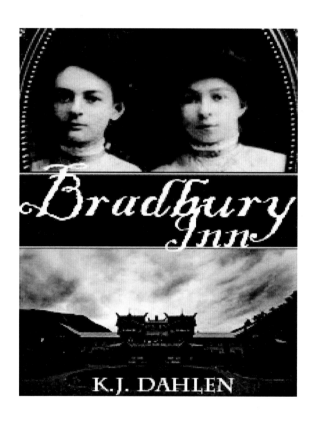

I'd like to dedicate this book to: My daughter-in-law Jessie and my son -in- law Jamey, you both have become a welcomed part of our hearts and family

Part I

Chapter One

As Jillian levy left the town of Brandenburg, Illinois she turned right at the intersection of highway 13. She spent the whole morning with her real estate agent, signing the necessary papers to become the owner of the Bradbury Inn. The Inn was all that was left of an old plantation called, Bradbury Archers.

She found several historical facts very interesting about the place, one of them being it had been a stop on the Underground Railroad for runaway slaves. As close as the plantation was to the Mississippi River the slaves would board the ships taking wheat up to the northern states. From there they would travel overland to their final destinations.

The plantation was built in the early 1700's and run as an Inn from 1900 until the 1930's. The Inn belonged to the same family that ran the plantation for generations, the Bradbury family.

Jillian turned off the highway onto a private road and continued up the driveway. At first glance the Inn looked a little lonely and out of place. She could see that someone had started restoration of the old Inn but it hadn't been finished yet.

The front façade of the building had been restored to the original specs but she knew from the realtor that the work hadn't been completed. Bradbury Inn had been owned and operated as a rooming house in the 1930's by a pair of sisters Claire and Matilda Bradbury. They were spinsters and the property had been left to them by their Father, Thomas Bradbury. Thomas had inherited the property from his father's family. Several generations owned and operated the property since its plantation days but only one other person operated it since the tragedy of 1931 and they hadn't lasted very long.

Tragedy to the Inn and the sisters came in the form of a man named Matthew Nixen in 1931. One of the rumors floating around Brandenburg said that Matilda fell in love with Matthew but Matthew fell in love with Claire and in a jealous rage Matilda burned the Inn down, trapping all three inside. Another said Matthew was in love with Matilda and it was Claire who started the fire. But when the fire had died down there were only two bodies found. What happened to the third body was anyone's guess. Since that time the Inn has been haunted by the pair of lovers and the jealous, vengeful sister.

Jillian was drawn to the Inn by a letter she had found in her late Grandmother's possessions. It was a letter from Matilda, written in 1930 before the fire that consumed the Inn and its occupants. The letter wasn't the jealous ramblings of a woman possessed, but a plea for help. However before help could arrive the fire burned the Inn and three souls were trapped forever. She also found a letter her grandmother had started to write to her friend Tilly but she never finished the letter.

Now Jillian had come to discover the truth. The last thing her Grandmother had asked her to do before she died was to find the truth about what happened that fateful day. Her grandmother had always been bothered by the fact she hadn't responded to Tilly's letter. She knew there was nothing she could do for Tilly now but her grandmother wanted to justify Tilly's death. She always told Jillian it wouldn't have been Tilly's way to hurt anyone else, not even her own sister. She and Matilda had once been close friends and Jillian listened with awe when her grandmother had told her tales of their escapades as young women in the days of post WWI.

Her Grandmother had died before Jillian could look into the matter but she believed in fulfilling her promises. When she'd come here to look into the matter everyone she spoke to tried to convince her the old Inn was haunted but Jillian didn't believe them. She heard several conflicting stories and decided to check it out herself. She bought the old Inn and decided to move in and see what all the fuss was about. Jillian was a writer and this story intrigued her so she was killing two birds with one stone, or at least she thought she was. The longer she stood there staring at the building in front of her, the more aware she became of a different sort of feeling. She had the feeling she was being watched. Staring at the Inn she couldn't see anyone but the feeling persisted.

As she approached the path to the front door she

noticed the front gate had rotted off its hinges but someone had set it up against the rest of the fence. The picket fence around the yard was weathered and broken, another sign of general abandonment around the Inn. Jillian grabbed the file and her overnight bag and whistled for her dog, Brandy to come and together they climbed the steps to the front door of the Inn. The front porch of the building wrapped around the entire front of the Inn. She had to step carefully as some of the boards on the steps and porch needed repairs.

There were gaping holes all over the porch and the whole Inn suffered from neglect. When she got to the front door the feeling of being watched got stronger. She paused for a moment before she unlocked the door to look around the yard. The yard was overgrown and unkempt. There were spots of color here and there but most of the flowers had died from neglect. There were clusters of green where the grass was overgrown but more so were large areas of brown were the lawn had suffered from disease and being overgrown.

She could only imagine how lush this area had once been. No one had lived here in years, but someone had tried to spruce it up. She could see where the lawn had been mowed not too long ago. Jillian shrugged and turned to the task at hand. She put aside the creepy feeling she was getting and unlocked the front door. The door groaned as she pushed it open and stepped inside. The air was thick with dust and a stale closed up smell.

The front parlor was styled to the 1920's era. All

the furniture was Victorian and the doilies on the back of the high backed sofas and chairs were yellowed with age. The front desk reminded Jillian of a bar but the wood was yellowed with age and had a thick layer of dust. Jillian had read that the previous owners, Mike and Sandy Pruitt tried to restore the Inn but couldn't finish it because of supernatural interference. The real estate agent that sold her the Inn had tried to steer away from the haunted aspect but Jillian hadn't been turned off. She asked about what happened and the agent had reluctantly told her some of the stories.

Jillian shivered. She didn't believe in ghosts but she did feel there was something here that didn't belong. She looked down at Brandy and said, "Well girl, are we ready for this?" Brandy just cocked her head to one side and looked at Jillian. Jillian smiled and rubbed her dog on the top of the head. She wasn't too keen on having ghosts or whatever haunted the Inn around her but she was determined to find out what happened here all those years ago.

The writer inside her wanted to know the juicy details but the woman inside her wanted to know what the story was between Matthew Nixen and the two women. She had a feeling the whole story hadn't been told yet. The feeling she had earlier regarding being watched was even stronger now that she was inside the Inn. She shivered as her imagination heated up.

She moved over to the desk area and noted the surroundings. The round braided rug under the table looked brand new. There was a cubby section behind the desk and each cubby had room for a key and mail if the occupant got any. The wallpaper was starting to curl around the edges and it too was yellowing with age. Jillian could almost imagine how grand the Inn must have been in its heyday. The floors would have been polished until they sparkled, and the woodwork around the parlor would have gleamed in the sunshine. The windows would have been polished to let all the sunshine in the lobby. Fresh flowers from the gardens would have been set out on the many tables adorning the Inn. The two sisters would have kept everything tidy and neat.

But now the Inn looked tired and not so neat and clean. Jillian believed a house had a soul; that it was a living breathing thing and the things that happened in the house left its own imprint on the house. Whatever tragedy happened here all those years ago had left its own mark within the Inn. According to all the stories, the Inn burns to the ground every year and every year it came back to life. That was the real story Jillian came to find out about.

Jillian looked toward the staircase to the left of the lobby. The grand staircase leading upstairs was carpeted and led to the landing on the second floor where most of the boarding rooms were located. As she climbed the staircase she recalled the stories she'd heard about this place and she recalled there were ten rooms in all, seven rooms upstairs and three downstairs. As she got to the top of the steps she could see the rooms were open, all but one that was. The far corner room door was closed.

Jillian wondered whose room the closed door belonged to. Was it Claire's room or Matilda's? Or maybe it was Matthew's room. According to the rumors that's where Matilda found the couple. It was said that she opened the door and found them in bed and in a jealous rage she locked the door and started a fire trapping Claire and Matthew inside. But that was just a rumor.

Claire and Matthew tried to get out but the door wouldn't open and all three lost their lives that day. The town's people were able to put out the fire but when they recovered the bodies they could only find Claire and Matthew. No one ever found Matilda's body. And that was part of the mystery of the Inn.

Jillian looked at the closed door again. Mike and Sandy Pruitt had left a message with the realtor that they hadn't been able to open that door. The realtor found that odd since the rest of the Inn had been easily accessible. Jillian knew there was something behind that door that wasn't meant to be seen and when the time was right, the door would open to reveal the final secret of the Inn.

She glanced down at the parlor again and decided that it was time to freshen up the place. She still had a few hours of daylight left so she went back downstairs and walked over to the windows and snapped up the shades. The overcast skies had cleared and now sunlight filled the room. She could see particles of dust floating everywhere. She opened the windows and breathed deeply as the cool fresh air came inside.

It was early evening when she finished cleaning the

parlor. After almost seventy years of neglect the place looked pretty good. She couldn't find any signs of the fire that supposedly destroyed the Inn. She didn't know who rebuilt the Inn and no one in town did either. They claimed that was part of the haunting. One day the Inn burned to the ground and the next day the Inn was back in all its fading glory. It was one of the reason people were afraid to come here.

Sitting down on one of the stairs Jillian noticed that Brandy had made herself comfortable on the braided rug underneath the round table. She was snoozing in the last bit of sunlight coming through the open door. Twisting open the cap of a water bottle she viewed the parlor. It looked clean and ready for someone to come inside. She glanced over at the round table again and frowned.

She had dusted it earlier but when she looked at it just now the dust was back. She got up and walked over to the table. In the dust someone had written the words, *"Get out while you can."*

Jillian shivered at the cryptic message. The hairs on the back of her neck tingled and she had goose bumps on the back of her arms. She glanced around the parlor. There wasn't anyone else in the house and the Inn was at the end of a long dirt road. The town of Brandenburg was five miles away. It was possible that someone had entered the Inn while she was busy opening up one of the rooms upstairs but she hadn't heard Brandy bark and she hadn't heard a car outside so she knew that no one had come in. The words made no sense to her. Why would anyone try to frighten her away? Was this part of the haunting?

There was no mention of any trouble associated with vandals or anything else. The people of the town nearby wanted nothing to do with the Inn. Most of them kept away from the place.

Jillian started to shake her head at her fanciful thoughts of ghosts when a door slammed shut upstairs. She frowned and went to investigate the noise. Brandy jumped up at the noise and followed her up the stairs. She got to the top of the stairs and saw the third door down was closed. She walked toward the door and turned the handle. The door swung open easily enough and Jillian couldn't see anything wrong inside the room. She shrugged and thought that maybe the wind had blown the door closed. She walked over to the window and closed it. She had opened it earlier to air out the place. Jillian looked down at the dog and shook her head.

"I must be tired. That's the only thing that makes any sense. If someone had been here you would have let me know." She fondled the dog's ears. "Come on Brandy; let's go get something to eat. I don't know about you but I'm getting hungry."

Brandy's tail wagged in response and Jillian turned. The corner of her eye caught a movement at the end of the hall and she slowly turned her head to look at what it was while Brandy started to growl. For a brief moment in time Jillian could have sworn that a woman was standing there but before she could make out the woman's face she disappeared. Fear flashed in Jillian. It started in her chest and grew as it spread through her abdomen. She closed her eyes and opened them again. Looking at the end of the hall she saw nothing.

She looked at Brandy and the dog looked back at her. Her tail was wagging and she butted Jillian's hand. Jillian responded by rubbing her head. She felt as if she was going crazy. She had seen a woman standing there and Brandy had started to growl but whatever Brandy had felt it was gone now. Jillian shook her head. She didn't know what was going on.

"Come on girl, let's go eat." Jillian felt a little silly. She had been hearing too many ghost stories and it convinced her that the Inn really was haunted, she decided after thinking about it for a moment.

Making her way to the kitchen Jillian rummaged through the refrigerator for something to eat. She had had the water and power turned on a few days before and had brought some food with her. She would have to go and get more food in a few days, but for tonight she had enough. Sitting on a chair she began eating a sandwich as she watched Brandy scarf down her supper. In front of her on the table was the file she had brought with her. In the file was her grandmother's letter, an old photograph and a file of information on the Inn. Jillian had done a little research on the history of the Inn before she got here. Most of what she knew about the Inn was in the file.

The photograph had been taken in front of the Inn back in 1931. It was a photograph of her Grandfather and Grandmother standing outside with Claire and Matilda

Bradbury. Her grandmother told her that Matthew Nixen himself had taken the photo and it had been taken just weeks before the fire had destroyed everything.

Jillian opened the file and found the letter. The flowery handwriting belonged to Matilda and it bespoke of a time long ago. As she read the words written to her grandmother she couldn't help but feel she was intruding on something between two very good friends...

"My dear friend Chloe,

It hasn't been that long since you and you're dear husband were here on your honeymoon yet so much has happened since you left. I have fallen in love for the first time and I must agree it is something very special. You told me it was a special feeling but never having known true love I wasn't sure if I believed it or not. Now I know you were telling the truth. I want to shout my feeling from the rooftops but my dear Matthew dislikes open displays of emotions.

I thought at first he rather liked my sister Claire but it was me he has come to care for. You know that if he really cared for her I would be devastated and of course not show my feelings but it is me he cares for and I couldn't be happier.

Claire will of course be devastated when we run away together but when we return in a few weeks she will understand why we did it this way. I would never hurt her for any reason but I must have Matthew for my own.

I must tell you that when Matthew first arrived I

pegged him as a scoundrel. I mistakenly thought he was a man just looking for a wealthy woman to support him, but that was before I got to know him. I also thought he was going to fall for Claire as she is the oldest of us and it is up to her to marry first, that's part of the reason we have to elope. Claire would be humiliated if I got married first.

Wish me happiness.
Matilda

Jillian closed the file and thought about the letter. From all accounts she had heard it was Matilda catching Claire and Matthew together that started the troubles. Why then would Matilda write her grandmother that she and Matthew were running away together? One of the reasons she was here was to discover the truth about what really happened, if she could. Her grandmother had told her that the girls always kept diaries and if she could find them she would find the truth. This house held many secrets and it was up to her to find them.

Chapter Two

Jillian shrugged and looked down at Brandy. The dog was looking back at her. "What do you think Brandy? Are the diaries still here somewhere? If they are will they help solve the mystery of the fire and the tangled love triangle between Matthew, Claire and Matilda?" Brandy cocked her head to one side and just looked at Jillian.

Jillian smiled. "If only you could talk, huh girl? I feel a little silly talking to myself all the time." She leaned forward and rested her head on the dog's head. When she lifted her head, she asked Brandy, "Shall we call it a night? I have to find somewhere to sleep anyway and tomorrow is a new day."

She got up and tidied the kitchen. When she got to the parlor she looked outside. The evening sun was fading from the horizon and everything was quiet. She went around and closed up the windows and as she was about to close the front door Brandy raced through it.

Jillian frowned as she watched the dog run into the wooded area next to the driveway. She called out, "Brandy, here girl." But Brandy didn't return. Jillian hadn't seen whatever it was that Brandy had chased into the woods but she knew the dog would be back.

Jillian sat down on the front porch for a while waiting for Brandy to return. It was so peaceful here Jillian felt she had stepped back in time to a forgotten time where everything didn't run by the clock. She could actually hear the crickets and the tree frogs sitting here. While she sat there she couldn't stop thinking about the letter Matilda had written. She wondered what had gone so terribly wrong all those years ago. Had Claire felt the sting of betrayal or had Matilda? Which one of the sisters had Matthew Nixen really loved? All the possibilities running threw her head were giving her a headache.

It was completely dark outside when Brandy returned. Jillian hadn't really noticed the time until she felt Brandy's cold wet nose nudge her she had been lost in her own thoughts.

She patted the dog's head and they went inside. The evening air had grown cool and when Jillian closed the door and turned the lock she shivered. It was too late to do any more tonight so she climbed the stairs to go to bed. Earlier in the day when she had been opening the upstairs she had placed her overnight bag in the room at the top of the steps and it was there where she and Brandy would sleep tonight.

When Jillian went into the room she felt a chill in the air. Rubbing the back of her arms she went over to check the window but it was shut. She frowned as she looked around the room. Nothing was out of place but there was something different. The room was colder than the rest of the Inn. Brandy went toward the closet door and Jillian noticed it was open slightly.

She went toward the door in question and wondered

how it came to be open. She opened it all the way and found nothing inside. Jillian frowned and reached for the string to turn on the light. The light didn't reveal anything unusual and when she went to turn the light off, Jillian noticed a piece of wallpaper was torn away from the wall at the top of the inside wall. She stepped inside the closet for a better look.

In the top right hand corner of the small closet the wall paper was loose. When Jillian pulled on it a bit it came away easily from the wall. Behind the paper there was a little alcove and inside the alcove were a several small notebooks.

Jillian took one of the books down from its hiding place and took it out into the bedroom for a better look. She sat down on the bed and opened the book. At first she didn't realize what the book was but the more she read it the more she was convinced that the book was one of the sisters' missing diaries.

She flipped to the first page of the book and found which of the sisters' the book belonged to. It was Claire's diary. Jillian went back into the closet and got the rest of the books. *"Ask and ye shall receive."* She muttered to herself. The ease in which she found the first set of diaries astounded her. It was almost as if they were waiting for her to discover them. Jillian shivered as she sat down on the bed again and began to read the first book.

***

She must have fallen asleep at one point because the

next thing she knew Brandy was at the door growling softly. Jillian got up and went to the door and pressing her ear against the door she listened.

She could hear voices raised in anger somewhere down the hall. She couldn't make out the words, but she could sense the feeling of anger present. Then she heard footsteps running toward her room. Brandy heard them too and she began barking.

Jillian hushed her and tried to listen but she didn't hear anything. She pressed her lips together and reached for the doorknob. Opening the door just enough to peek out in the hall Jillian was surprised to see there wasn't anyone there. Frowning she opened the door completely and stepped out of the bedroom. The hallway was empty.

Taking hold of Brandy's collar she and the dog walked down to the end of the hall. The Inn was empty but Jillian knew she heard voices as well as footsteps. Was someone playing a trick on her?

On the way back to her bedroom she checked every room but found nothing out of place. She got to her room and found nothing there as well. She shook her head and got undressed. She placed Claire's diaries on the table beside the bed and shut off the lights. She was too tired to read anymore tonight.

Chapter Three

Early the next morning as the sunlight shone into her window Jillian groaned and tried to turn over. Her hand flopped down over the edge of the bed and Brandy touched it with her nose. The wet sensation of the dog's nose startled Jillian awake and she groaned again. After the mysterious happenings of the night before, it had taken her a long time to fall asleep.

She sat up and glanced over at the diaries and was surprised to find them still there. She wouldn't have been at all surprised to find them missing but she knew that if someone had come into her room, Brandy would have alerted her.

She got up; dressed and gathering the books together she went downstairs. Letting Brandy out the front door, Jillian went to the kitchen to make a pot of coffee. While she waited for the coffee to brew she began reading the diary again. Last night she had gotten to the part just before Matthew arrived.

Claire had described life in the late 1920's, living with her sister in the business their father had left them. While respectable she longed for a little adventure and romance. Claire had been yearning for an adventure that would sustain her through the mundane, something she could remember during the lonely nights in her dreams. She wanted, no yearned for something she knew no respectable woman should have.

She felt her soul crying out but she didn't dare dream for too much and Claire wanted just a hint of danger in her life. She was already twenty five and didn't have a husband. She sounded a bit like Jillian. Jillian got the feeling there was something going on that Claire hadn't told anyone else about. She had hinted that there might be someone in her life but Jillian was confused. Matthew hadn't arrived at the Inn yet.

Jillian took a break to let Brandy back in the house and to get a cup of coffee. Sitting down again she couldn't help herself, she had to pick up the diary again. She wanted to know what Claire felt about the man that would eventually lead her sister to run away with him.

Jillian was growing more and more concerned for someone she'd never met as she continued to read the words Claire Bradbury wrote. Her coffee grew cold as she read about Matthew's arrival and the feelings that both sister's shared for the man Matilda described as a scoundrel.

Claire was very graphic as her words filled the pages. Jillian could understand her fears and her longings for the man that she described in her diary. The words she read were feelings she had never experienced before and as she described them Jillian thought about the betrayal Claire would have felt had Matilda run away with the man Claire loved.

Jillian finished one book and picked up the next one

and shook her head. Claire had written that passion had overtaken the young couple and they had given into their growing love for one another as only a man and a woman could. Jillian couldn't believe what she was reading.

Claire was having an affair with the man Matilda loved! Claire went on to say that she knew how Matilda felt about Matthew and how Matthew didn't want to hurt Matilda but it was Claire that he really loved. He proved it every time they were together.

Jillian was so engrossed in what she was reading that when Brandy stuck her nose on her arm Jillian was startled. She looked over at Brandy and Brandy wagged her tail.

"Dog, I swear you gave me a fright. What's the matter, are you hungry?" Jillian asked the dog. "I guess I am too." She got up and went to the refrigerator and got some bread out. She made toast for herself and opened a can of dog food for Brandy.

She warmed her coffee and thought about what the diary told her about Claire. Was it possible that Matthew was playing both women for fools? Or was it possible that neither of them knew they had both fallen for the same man? Jillian decided that she needed to see if she could find Matilda's diaries. This drama was intriguing to say the least and maybe if she could find Matilda's diaries she would find out more about the fire.

Jillian hadn't made up her mind about Matthew yet. Maybe he was the scoundrel Matilda and Claire first thought he was or maybe he really loved one of them but the question was, which sister did he really love? Now there were more questions than answers and Jillian needed to know what the truth was. And she wondered who the mystery man in Claire's life had been and what happened to him? Would he play a part in what ultimately happened the night of the fire?

After she ate her toast Jillian picked up the diary again. The next several pages were dedicated to the growing love Claire felt for the man that had become her lover. Jillian skipped over the ramblings and got to the next part. It seemed that Matilda found them together. Claire wrote that she would never forget the look of betrayal on her sister's face when she found them. Nor would she forget the scream that shattered her soul.

Claire wrote:

"My secret is no longer a secret. Tilly caught Matthew and me together today. I didn't realize until it was too late that she too had strong feelings for Matthew until I saw the look on her face. I felt like such a fool. Tilly screamed when the shock had passed and it was the sound of her own heart breaking. She ran away and Matthew ran after her but it was too late. I don't know how I'm ever going to face her again.

That was the last entry in the diary. Jillian put the diary down and got up to get some more coffee. She couldn't help herself. She was caught up in someone else's life and she couldn't stop wondering how much time passed between that last entry and the fire that destroyed the Inn. Had the fire happened that night or days later?

She had a feeling she would only find out if she found Matilda's diaries. Jillian glanced up at the ceiling and wondered which of the remaining rooms upstairs was Matilda's. What about the sounds she had heard last night? Were they somehow connected to the mystery of the fire?

Jillian found herself climbing the stairs and going from room to room in search of something that would tell her that the room belonged to Matilda Bradbury. She searched each room thoroughly until she came to the last room in the hall, the one with the door that wouldn't open for the Pruitt's.

Jillian had a creepy feeling about this room. She had to take a deep breath and reaching for the door knob she tried to turn it but she found it wouldn't turn. Jillian squatted and looked at the handle. There didn't seem to be any obstruction in the lock. Jillian tried it again but the door was truly stuck shut.

She was determined to get inside the room. She went back downstairs and around to the back of the house. Jillian could see the bedroom window and the glass was black. It wasn't the same as the others but then the others had been replaced when the Pruitt's owned the Inn. She wondered why they hadn't changed this window.

Jillian went to the garage in search of a ladder. She found one lying along the side of the garage and she carried it over to the bedroom window. Climbing up the ladder she found herself looking to a bedroom. There was a big bed in the middle of the room and everything in the room told her that this was Tilly's room. A suitcase was open on the bed and she could see there were clothes packed inside. On the bed were at least two piles of clothes that needed to be packed yet.

Drawers in the dresser were left open and the closet door was still open. The room looked as if someone had just left and was coming back to finish packing.

She wondered what had happened to delay the packing and why the door wouldn't open. She tried to lift the window sash and was surprised when it slid open under her hand. She pushed the window up as far as she could and climbed up the last bars of the ladder to gain entry into the room.

It smelled musty and dusty in there but there was no sign of the fire that had destroyed the Inn. She had yet to find any sign of the fire that was supposed to have destroyed the Inn and she was beginning to have doubts about there being a fire at all.

This room had either been spared from the flames or protected from it. Protected by what was anybody's guess. Jillian looked around the room. She went over to the open suitcase on the bed and looked inside. There was a beautiful white linen dress lying on the top. She touched the fabric and it felt smooth. Jillian moved over to the closet and opened the door.

This closet was similar to the one in Claire's room and Jillian checked the wall paper for any tears. She was disappointed when she didn't find any. Her eyes went back to the suitcase on the bed.

Was it possible if Matilda was leaving that she

would take the diaries with her? Jillian went back to the bed and began taking the clothes out of the suitcase. Piling them up neatly on the bed she discovered that Matilda was indeed taking the diaries with her. Jillian found four handsomely bound books on the bottom of the case.

She went over to the door and tried to open it from this side but she couldn't get the door to move. Tucking the books under her arm she went over to the window and climbed back down the ladder. It was trickier trying to hang on to the books at the same time but she got to the ground.

Going back around to the front of the house she sat down on the porch and opened the first book. It was as she expected, Matilda's diary. Jillian wanted to skip the parts that didn't deal with Matthew but she knew if she did she wouldn't get the whole story. She wanted to know Matilda as well as she felt she knew Claire.

As she read the entries Jillian noticed a distinct difference in the two women. Claire was more of a dreamer while Matilda was more down to earth. Matilda had no illusions of grandeur and she spoke of herself as less than beautiful but all that changed when Matthew came to stay with them.

Matilda spoke of how she didn't trust Matthew Nixen and how she thought him nothing more than a ladies man:

"I don't trust him." She wrote. *"His eyes bespoke of more knowledge about life than he himself lets on. I can see my sister is becoming infatuated with his stories of his travels and such nonsense. But it's his eyes that have*

captured my attention. They are of a color not usually associated with eye color. I've never seen eyes the color of lavender blooms in summer time. They often change from lavender to gray without warning."

Jillian frowned at the description of Matthew's eye color. Her words said one thing but her description said something else entirely. She continued to read…

"Matthew Nixen is probably nothing more than a scoundrel waiting and hoping that either my sister or I will give him the time of day. He looks at the world through weary eyes and I think he's looking for a soft place to lay his head, away from the worries and troubles of the world outside these walls. I can't help but be wary of his attentions and yet… I have to wonder what it would be like to be held in his arms and kissed. He has the loveliest lips I've ever seen on anyone."

Jillian raised her eyebrows and laughed out loud. Matilda might not think of herself as a dreamer but her words betrayed her as one. Jillian turned another page.

"Matthew has found out my secret desire for him and I fear he will exploit it or worse yet… he will tell my sister about my desire for him and they would share a fine joke on me. I have noticed that they have become close, closer than I would care for."

Jillian shook her head. Matilda didn't know her sister very well. Claire never would have laughed at her feelings. The sisters had been very close, often sharing each other's dreams and desires. They had grown up together to complement each other, a way of life often missing in today's way of life. Jillian wished she could have met the sisters and Matthew for herself. She had a feeling she would have liked all three of them.

She went to the kitchen to make herself a sandwich. As she came through the doorway she happened to look up and she gasped in fear. There was a black aura in the corner of the kitchen. It seemed to hover briefly and then it was gone. Jillian felt a shiver of something unexplainable. It raised the hairs on the back of her neck. She turned around and went back outside to the porch. Sitting down in the chair she had to remember to breathe. Brandy looked up at her from her spot on the porch and cocked her head at Jillian.

Jillian took a couple of deep breathes and exhaled slowly several times. She turned her head to stare in the general direction of the doorway to the kitchen. She got up and went back inside. Brandy got up and followed her into the house. Jillian felt comforted by the presence of her dog and she grasped Brandy's collar and lead her to the kitchen door.

Jillian waited for Brandy's reaction to the kitchen door before she moved forward. Glancing around she didn't notice anything out of place, nor did she find anything that shouldn't have been there before. When she turned and looked in the corner she saw the black aura and it was gone, almost like it had never been there.

Jillian tightened her grip on the dog's collar and moved forward into the room. Sweeping her gaze she found nothing to be afraid of anywhere. She let go of Brandy's collar and felt foolish for imagining the worst.

"There is nothing here to be afraid of," Jillian spoke the words out loud. Her voice echoed in the empty Inn. When Jillian didn't hear or see anything else, she didn't know if that fact offered her comfort or not. She had seen the black aura a few minutes ago and now she didn't.

She went about the task of making a sandwich and a glass of iced tea and took her lunch out to the back porch. She looked around the back yard as she ate her food. Her mind was busy thinking about Tilly and Claire.

Then a noise caught her ear and she looked off into the distance. Brandy had run off a few minutes ago and she could see her barking at something in the distance. Jillian got up to investigate. As she walked to Brandy she took note of the beauty around her. She walked about ten minutes before she found Brandy waiting for her just outside an old cemetery plot surrounded by a low picket fence. The fence had at one time been painted but age and weather had stripped the paint off most of the wood.

Jillian looked at Brandy and said, "I wonder who's buried here? Shall we find out?" Jillian stepped over the low fence and Brandy jumped over it. Here the grass was longer and the cemetery plot hadn't been tended in years. She made her way to the mass of headstones in the center of the plot. She began pulling weeds and tall grass to clear the headstones. Brushing the debris away she began reading the names carved on the stones.

"Thomas Eugene Bradbury, Beloved Father and

Husband. Mary Ellen Bradbury, Beloved Wife and Mother, Ian Bradbury, Loribelle Bradbury." Jillian noted that Ian and Loribelle died as young children in the early 1920's. She continued to pull the long grass until she could see all the headstones. The oldest headstone belonged to Jeremiah Bradbury. His date of death was 1758 and beside him lay his wife and seven children. There were other family members but she couldn't find any headstones for Matilda or Claire. She sat down nearby and stared at the headstones. She couldn't help but wonder why the sisters weren't buried in the family plot.

She sat there most of the afternoon. When she got up to go she had weeded almost the entire plot. Jillian felt it was the right thing to do. When she started back to the house she looked down at her hands. They were dirty and sore from pulling so much long grass but she was satisfied with what she had gotten done.

As she came up to the back door she peeked inside the kitchen warily. She didn't see anything out of the ordinary so she went inside. Walking over to the sink she began washing her hands. Brandy came inside the kitchen and plopped herself down on the floor.

Jillian glanced at her dog and sighed. "You are supposed to be my guard dog. How can you possibly guard me if you keep taking off on me?"

Jillian knelt down and began rubbing Brandy's head and behind her ears. Brandy responded by leaning into her caress. Brandy whimpered her pleasure briefly then her ears perked up and she turned her head toward the front door.

Jillian stood up as the sound of another car coming down the road caught her ears. She walked through the house to the front porch as another car pulled into the parking lot and parked next to her car. Jillian waited for the driver to exit and when he did she found herself looking at a stranger. He was tall and dark haired and for a moment he simply stared at her. Then the passenger side door opened and the stranger walked around the car and helped an old man out. He too was tall but his hair was white and he walked with the aid of a cane and the arm of the younger man.

They walked toward the front porch and when they stopped, the older man looked up at her and he had the most particular look on his face. He tried to say something but found he couldn't. He simply stared at her in shock.

Jillian glanced at the younger man and back to the old man and asked, "Can I help you?"

The younger man smiled and nodded. "I know this is a strange request but my uncle would like to have a look around the Inn. You see he stayed here once a long time ago and he wants to look around it again before he dies."

Jillian's eyebrows shot way up in her forehead. "His name wouldn't happen to be Matthew Nixen would it?" she muttered a little louder than she had planned.

Chapter Four

The younger man tilted his head a bit and told her, "Why yes it is actually. How did you know that?"

Jillian was stunned. She had been told that Matthew Nixen died here a long time ago. "Who are you exactly?" she asked.

"Can my uncle sit down while we chat? He is an old man and he can't stand for too long a time anymore."

Jillian motioned for them to come up the steps and she pointed to a couple of chairs on the other side of the porch. When Matthew Nixen was seated his nephew looked over at Jillian and stated why they were there.

"I don't know if you know the story behind the Inn."

"I know one story at least." Jillian interrupted him. She looked over at Matthew and frowned. "Your uncle was supposed to have died almost eighty years ago along with the sisters who ran this place. He was supposed to have burned to death with them."

The young man nodded. "Yes I know." He stuck out his hand. "My name is Seth Nixen by the way. Uncle Matthew barely escaped the fire that night. He had been run out of the Inn just a few hours before the fire started. A man named George Walker knocked him out and drove him about a mile away and dumped him along the highway.

When my uncle came too he walked back to the Inn. When he got back here he saw the place was on fire. He tried to get back into the house to make sure the sisters got out alright but the flames were too high. The sisters didn't make it out I'm afraid. The town folks found two bodies in the rubble the next day."

"Your uncle must be a very old man by now. The fire happened in 1931." Jillian stated.

Seth nodded. He was picking up on the hostility in her voice and he didn't know why it was there. "My uncle is a very old man. He just turned 104 last week. The doctors didn't really want him to come this far but he insisted on coming here."

"Why?" Jillian asked.

Seth shook his head. "I'm not really sure. He wouldn't give anyone an explanation. He just said he had to come."

Jillian looked at her unwanted guests and nodded. "Maybe he can answer some questions while he's here." She got up and went inside. Seth helped his uncle to his feet and helped him inside.

"You look just like my Tilly." Matthew told her as she brushed past him on her way inside.

Jillian stopped in her tracks and looked at him. "What? What did you say?"

The old man looked at her with the same lavender eyes Matilda had described in her diary. "I said that you look just like my Tilly. She was a beautiful woman too."

Jillian looked at him and then looked at Seth. Seth

just shook his head. "He rambles a lot." He offered in explanation.

Jillian walked into the front parlor and turned to see his face when he came face to face with the past. Matthew Nixen walked slowly into the room. His eyes darted around as if remembering each and every corner of the room. He glanced to the room at the top of the stairs and then turned to the room at the end of the hall. Tears were rolling down his face as he remembered that both Claire and Matilda died eighty years ago.

Seth helped his uncle over to the sofa in the corner of the room. Suddenly the door behind them slammed shut. Both Seth and Jillian looked at the door briefly before looking at each other. There was something in the air that both of them could feel. There was tension and something else, something they couldn't identify.

Matthew smiled and chuckled a bit. "Claire doesn't like the fact that I came back." He muttered.

"Excuse me?' Jillian asked as she twirled around to face him. "What did you say?"

Matthew waved his hand around the room. "Can't you tell the girls are still here? Well their spirits are anyway and right now Claire isn't happy with the fact that I came back."

Seth looked pained. "Uncle Matthew, you know that's not so. Once a person dies, their spirits are gone. Ghosts aren't real."

Jillian smiled. "Oh I don't know about that. I think when someone is murdered or killed before it's their time to go, I think the spirit can stay here on earth until some sort of closure or justice is done."

Matthew nodded. "I always told Tilly I would come back for her someday."

A cold breeze brushed past Jillian and manifested in the form of a woman in front of Matthew. Seth backed away slowly and came to stand beside the equally stunned Jillian.

Matthew smiled at the figure of the woman in front of him. "Hello Claire." He said.

Claire narrowed her eyes. "Why did you come back here Matthew? Why after all these years?"

"I came back to get my Tilly. You told me a long time ago that she didn't want me anymore and that she had run away and for the longest time I believed what you said."

"But…" She commented. "You suddenly don't believe me anymore?" Why not?"

"Because I finally admitted to myself what I should have believed all those years ago. Something happened just before I left, just before the fire. You did something to Matilda and I came back to find out what it was."

Claire threw her head back and laughed. It was an eerie sounding laugh and it made the short hairs on the back of Jillian's arms stand up. Something was happening right here and right now. No one who wasn't a witness would ever believe what was going on.

Claire looked at Matthew and a cunning look came to her eyes. "I admit it. Tilly never ran away. She wouldn't have run away from here unless it was with you. She was quite besotted with you, you know, even after she caught the two of us together. She was still in love with you."

Matthew closed his eyes briefly. "That was a mistake and you know it. I never would have been in your bed to begin with. How did you manage that anyway? Getting me in bed with you at just the right time for Tilly to walk in a catch us?"

Claire chuckled. "It was so easy; any fool could have done it. All it took was a few drops of laudanum in your juice to make you feel woozy. I did have a heck of a time getting your clothes off and then I had to wait until the laudanum wore off a bit so you were almost conscious. The rest was as they say, easy as pie. Tilly walked in and the look on her face said it all."

Matthew shook his head. "Why Claire? Why would you do something as evil as that to your own sister? All she ever did was love you. We weren't trying to hurt you."

Claire's face grew dark and her eyes glowed red. "I did it to you, you fool. I didn't want to hurt Tilly but she needed to see you for what you were."

"And what was I?" Matthew wanted to know. "What was I that you hated me so much that you would destroy what Tilly and I had together?"

"Claire loved you." Jillian told them. She'd read how much Claire had cared for Matthew. "Claire loved you and you didn't return her love. You cared for Matilda."

Claire turned and faced Jillian and Seth. Tears ran down her face as she nodded. "He was everything I ever wanted in a husband. He was kind and caring, gentle and strong. He should have been mine but my greedy sister stole him away from me. Well I fixed both of them that night. I got rid of Matthew and I tricked Matilda into thinking he was gone for good. Poor dear, she was inconsolable."

Matthew struggled to his feet. "What did you do to her, you evil witch? Where is my Tilly?"

Claire turned to Matthew. "You'll never find her. Her spirit is still here only because her final resting place has never been found. No one will ever find her. I made sure of that."

"What about the fire?" Jillian asked. "If Matthew was already gone and Tilly was dead, why did you burn the place to the ground? And who else was here that night? The papers said there were two bodies recovered that night. One man and one woman."

Claire remembered that night again and the look on her face was one of pure terror. "The fire was an accident. My little dog Sammy was chasing a squirrel and tipped over a lamp in the hallway. I was trapped in one of the rooms and I couldn't get out. The man was another tenant by the name of George Walker. He tried to get to me and the fire burned him alive. The Inn burned to the ground before anyone could get here."

"What about Tilly? Did the fire kill her as well?" Matthew asked with tears in his eyes.

Claire nodded and turned away. She shimmered for a moment then disappeared altogether. Her sobs could be heard by everyone. They sounded so forlorn.

Chapter Five

"I have a question. If the Inn burned down to the ground that night eighty years ago who rebuild it?" Jillian asked. "I mean someone had to rebuild it right? Otherwise it wouldn't be here today."

Matthew shook his head. "I forgot it's been so long ago." Matthew told her. "The place burned all those years ago but no one ever rebuilt it. One day all there was here was ashes and then the next morning the Inn suddenly reappeared. Everything was the way it was before the fire." Matthew paused to shake his head. "For years after that no one from town would come out here. Everyone was afraid the place was haunted."

"I can see where they would think that." Jillian told him. She had to know something. "The Inn just reappeared out of thin air, just as it was before the fire?"

Matthew nodded.

"That just seems so odd." Jillian said.

"I know. I stayed around this area for a while after the fire. I couldn't believe it either."

"Why do you suppose the Inn came back?" Jillian asked.

"I have a theory about that." Matthew spoke softly.

"Why do you think it came back?" Jillian asked.

"I think it came back because no one found Tilly." Matthew told them. "Every year the Inn burns to the ground and every year it comes back. We have to find where Tilly's body is."

No one spoke for the longest time then Seth looked at Jillian helplessly. "So now what?" he asked.

"We have to find Tilly." Matthew said quietly. "It's the only way to break this curse."

"What curse?" Seth asked.

Matthew looked at his nephew and smiled slightly. "The curse that's keeping me alive when I should have been dead a long time ago; the curse that's keeping Claire from crossing over and the same curse that's keeping Tilly a prisoner. She has to be in this house somewhere, we just have to find her."

Seth shook his head. "Uncle Matthew, for the last time, there is no curse."

"I wouldn't be too sure about that." Jillian told him.

"Come on don't tell me you believe in old wife's tales too?" Seth scolded.

"Did you ever happen to wonder where those old wife got their tales to tell?" Jillian asked. "In every tale there's just enough of the truth to keep the tale alive."

"Oh please." Seth whined as he rolled his eyes toward the ceiling. "I thought you were smarter than that."

"We need to find where Claire hid Tilly." Jillian told him.

"We need to hurry." Matthew said.

"Why?" Jillian and Seth asked together.

Matthew looked at them both. "The anniversary of night the fire burned the Inn to the ground is three days from now. I have a feeling deep in my bones that Claire is going to start another fire."

Jillian nodded. "Now that you've come back she just might." She hesitated and said, "Didn't Claire say her dog started the fire by overturning a lamp in the parlor?"

Matthew shook his head. "When I came back that night I found Sammy's body outside the Inn. The poor dog's neck was broken and it looked like someone had tossed her out the front door. There wasn't a singed hair on her head."

"Maybe we should stay for a few days." Seth suggested. "Just to make sure there's no trouble."

Jillian nodded. "I'll get some rooms ready. Suddenly I find I'm not all that anxious to be alone out here."

Jillian left to ready the rooms and Matthew gave his nephew an odd look. "I'm glad we're staying for a while. I feel there will be more trouble."

"What do you mean?" Seth asked.

"There's more than Claire's spirit roaming this house. I feel something more like hatred here." Matthew told him.

"Are you forgetting Tilly's spirit? You said she was here too." Seth reminded him.

Matthew shook his head. "My Tilly would never hurt anyone. She was and always will be a gentle woman; no this is someone else entirely."

"How do you know this?" Seth asked his uncle.

"I can feel it, deep down in my bones."

"But Uncle Matthew…" Seth began.

"No, I know it's true whether you believe it or not. There is something here that is evil." Matthew insisted.

Seth glanced at his uncle and noted he was sweating and pale. The whole trip had been more than he could take right now. Seth stood and reached for his uncle's arm, "Come on Matthew, let's find our room. I think you need to rest."

Matthew struggled to his feet and trudged behind Seth. When they got to the stairs they saw Jillian coming down.

She smiled at Seth and said, "I made Matthew a room downstairs. I hope you don't mind."

Matthew smiled at her and said, "My child I don't mind at all. I don't think I would have gotten up the stairs tonight."

Jillian grinned. "I had a feeling about that. I made up a room for your nephew right next to yours."

"Bless you child," Matthew told her. "I hope it wasn't any trouble."

"None at all, although I should warn you, I heard something last night, something I can't explain but it might be something from the past. I heard words of anger and footsteps running down the hall. Then there was nothing. I looked but I didn't see anything. I also saw a vision of the woman you called Claire. She was just standing at the end of the hall. I only caught sight of her for a moment and then she was gone." Jillian told them.

Matthew nodded. "This close to the anniversary I

wouldn't be surprised. The spirits of the dead are restless and often relive past events."

Jillian cocked her head and stared at him. "Do you know anything about it? The voices raised in anger I mean?"

Matthew nodded. "I might." He ambled over to the sofa and sat down again. He placed his cane directly in front of him and looked at her. "I haven't been completely honest with you."

"What does that mean?" Jillian wanted to know.

"After the Inn came back I stayed here for a while. I was the only person in the county that was actually brave enough to step inside the place," Matthew told her. "Anyway I stayed here for almost a year. Just before the anniversary of the fire I heard something in the night, much like you heard last night. A scene from the past played itself out, just as I remembered it. At first I didn't understand what was going on. That's when I realized that to break the curse I had to find Tilly. I had to free her soul. But before I could do that I found myself on the side of the road just as before. By the time I got back I could see the place was burning and I couldn't get back inside to look for them. I tried every year for five years and it always ended the same."

"I don't understand. The Inn burns down every year and then it comes back?" Jillian asked.

Matthew shook his head. "No, the fire isn't real, it only appears to be. But every year something or someone prevents me from getting back inside the Inn. I have to stand outside and watch the place burn to the ground. I have to listen to the god awful screams from that night. Finally after the fifth year I stopped coming back. It broke my heart but I couldn't relive the same tragedy every year. Everything from that night haunts my dreams and it always ends the same. I can't get back inside the Inn."

"Then why did you come back now?" Jillian wanted to know.

"I had a feeling this year I had to come back. I've lived too long and it was time to end the curse." Matthew told her. "I had to come back and find my Tilly."

"I keep trying to tell you Uncle Matthew, there is no curse." Seth stated as he turned to glare at Jillian, "And I wish you wouldn't keep on talking about ghosts and curses and other garbage."

"How do you explain Claire's visit?" Jillian asked. "You and I both saw her appear from nowhere and disappear into thin air."

Seth shrugged. "I don't know how to explain that but I don't believe in curses and other such nonsense."

Jillian hesitated briefly then told them, "I'm afraid there's more. Your uncle might be right about something evil being here."

"What do you mean?" Seth frowned.

"Earlier today I saw something that scared the socks right off me." She admitted.

"What was it?" Matthew asked.

"I was standing in the doorway to the kitchen and when I looked up there was a black aura shimmering in the corner." Jillian said. She shivered as she remembered the feeling that pulsated from the blackness. "I felt the cold and something else wash over me in waves. I thought the feelings were coming from the blackness but I could have been wrong. The longer I stared at the thing the stronger the feelings were. Finally when I was able to break off staring at it, it just disappeared."

"You felt trapped to the point you couldn't move." Matthew commented. "It wouldn't let you go and you were helpless, almost like being caught in a trap."

Jillian snapped her head to stare at him. "That's exactly how I felt. How did you know that?"

Matthew shook his head as he remembered something from his past. "Every year for five years I was caught by the same black cloud. When I woke up by the side of the road, I would hurry back here and I'd get just so close to the house and I would be surrounded by a black cloud. It stopped me in my tracks and would hold me while the Inn burned to the ground. I felt despair but I couldn't break free of the thing. It held me back and I was caught until the screaming stopped and the Inn was gone. Only then would I be able to move again. Only by then it was too late."

Chapter Six

Jillian shivered and looked at Seth. The expression on his face was one of disbelief. "I have a very hard time imagining such a thing." Seth muttered.

"Why?" Jillian asked.

Seth stood up and began to pace. "Why? Because any rational person wouldn't believe in ghosts and spirits. Any rational person doesn't believe in curses and buildings that magically reappear after being burnt to the ground."

"Yet here we are, standing in a building that was burnt to the ground eighty years ago." Jillian reminded him. "We all saw Claire appear and disappear. She was clearly not of this world and both your uncle and I saw the black cloud. We both felt its presence and its power. How do you as a rational person explain that?"

Seth stared at her for a moment. "Matthew is an old man with flights of fancy and I don't know anything about you but I would suggest you might be a little flighty yourself. As for Claire's appearance and disappearance, how do we know you didn't rig something up, in order to keep the haunting theme going?"

"Seth, that's enough." Matthew shouted. He struggled to his feet and shook his cane at his nephew. "You need to apologize to the young lady. She isn't part of any conspiracy. Whether you believe me or not I don't care. I lived through everything that happened all those years ago. I am not a doddering old fool and neither is she."

Seth glanced at Jillian. "I'm sorry if I offended you, but this is crazy stuff. I can't believe in something I can't see or rationalize. To my mind you are playing up to my uncle and I don't see the reason for it."

Jillian stood and nodded. "I accept your apology but I'll tell you something right now. I'm not playing games with anyone. I wouldn't know how or where to begin. I just bought the Inn two days ago. I am here trying to find out what happened all those years ago at the request of a very dear lady whom I loved very much. In fact your uncle might even remember her. Her name was Chloe Levy. She was here on her honeymoon eighty years ago." Jillian turned to Matthew and smiled.

"Of course I remember her." Matthew said. "Your grandmother was a lovely woman and your grandfather and I shared many a good time fishing and partaking of Tilly's father's homemade wine." Matthew chuckled. "Although the women never found the drink acceptable Jed and I found it quite tasty."

Jillian grinned. "Yes granddad liked a glass of wine once in a while." She reached out and laid her hand on Matthew's, "There is food in the kitchen if you get hungry later, please help yourself. Your rooms are the only ones made up on the main floor."

Matthew smiled at her. "Thank you for your kindness and your understanding. This hasn't been an easy trip for me."

Jillian turned her head to where Seth stood and

nodded. "I understand completely." She turned back to Matthew. "I hope you enjoy your stay." She turned and walked out to the front porch.

Matthew looked at his nephew and said, "Will you help me to my room, suddenly I'm very tired."

***

Jillian sat on the porch and watched the sunset. The sky was brilliant with colors tonight, ranging from gold to crimson. Her anger over Seth accusations was gone replaced with regret. She couldn't explain why regret and not hurt but it was regret inside her heart. As the evening sky slid into darkness she felt a chill. Glancing around the porch she didn't see anything out of the ordinary but she felt the chill get stronger.

Turning her head slightly to her left she saw a shimmering to her left. Jillian was afraid to move as the trees in the front of the Inn began to flutter. She stared at them as the wind began to call out, "Help me." The stronger the wind blew the more pronounced the words were. "Please help me. Tell Matthew to find the place where my bones are trapped. Please help me."

Then just as suddenly as the wind came up it died and the shimmering next to her was gone. Fear rooted Jillian to her seat. She turned her head toward the doorway and found herself looking into Seth's eyes. He too had heard the wind. She could tell by the paleness of his face. Without a word to her he turned and went back inside the

Inn.

Jillian got up and followed him. She found him in the kitchen sitting at the table. She busied herself making a pot of tea. When it was ready she grabbed two cups and brought it to the table. She poured them both a cup and sat down next to him.

Seth sat there for a long time fiddling with his cup. Without looking directly at her he made the comment, "My uncle is resting. It's been a long day for him."

"I imagine it has been an eventful day for him." Jillian said.

Seth turned his head and stared at her. "What just happened out there?"

Jillian shrugged. "If I had to hazard a guess I would have to say Tilly is asking for Matthew to rescue her."

"You heard it too, then?" Seth asked. Jillian nodded. "Is this real?" he asked. "I mean is this really for real?"

Jillian shrugged. "I'm not going to try and convince you of anything. Believe it not, it doesn't matter to me."

Seth stared at her for a moment then shook his head. "This is so far off the norm; even you have to admit that."

Jillian sipped her tea and didn't say anything. This was all new to her as well. "What do you want me to say? I've never come across this before either. My Grandmother asked me to come here and find out what happened so long ago. I never thought I'd run into this."

"What did you say?" Seth turned his head toward her.

Jillian nodded. "I came here because my grandmother was once a close friend of the sisters, in fact she came here on her honeymoon with my grandfather. That was about a couple of weeks before the fire that destroyed the Inn."

Jillian took a sip of her tea and went on, "My grandmother received a letter from Tilly saying that Tilly was in love with Matthew and they were running away together. My grandmother began a letter but was never able to finish or send it. By then the fire happened and both the sisters died. My grandmother always regretted not answering Tilly's letter and before she died she asked me to come here and find out what really happened."

"And what have you found out so far?" Seth asked.

"I found both of their diaries. It seems both women fell in love with your uncle. Claire's love was more lust but Tilly really did love him."

"And I really loved her." Came a voice from the door.

Jillian and Seth turned to find Matthew standing in the doorway. He came over to the table and sat down. He looked at both of them and said, "When I first arrived I wasn't looking for love or anything like it. I got back from the war in Europe a few years before and I couldn't shake what I saw and did over there. I couldn't keep a job and I felt lost. Now days they call it post-traumatic stress disorder but back then we didn't know what it was. I just wanted to get back to the way I was before the war.

"I came here looking for peace of mind. I found that

51

with Tilly. I tried to ignore what Claire was doing until the day I found myself in bed with her and Tilly saw us together. I don't think I'll ever forget the look of betrayal as long as I live. She looked shattered for want of a better word." He shook his head. "I wanted to kill Claire for what she'd done. I tried to explain to Tilly but she wouldn't speak to me. Later that night Claire came to me and told me Tilly was gone and I should go too."

Matthew was silent for a moment. "I was ejected from the Inn and dumped about a mile down the road. When I started back I got here just in time to find the Inn burning. I was too late. I had to stand out in the yard and watch the Inn burn to the ground."

For a moment no one said anything, and then Jillian said, "Tilly wants you to find her bones."

Matthew paled and turned to stare at her. "How do you know that?"

"She told us." Seth admitted.

Matthew looked at his nephew. "She told you? How? I mean the only one I've seen yet is Claire."

"Her words came to us on the winds." Jillian told him.

"She's still here then." Matthew said. "She's got to be here." Matthew struggled to his feet. "We have to find her. We have to. It's the only way to stop this curse."

Seth stood and steadied his uncle. "Then we'll find her but first you need to settle down." He helped his uncle back to his chair. "It's been a long day. I think we all need some rest."

Matthew nodded. "Maybe you're right. It has been a long day."

Chapter Seven

A little while later Jillian made her way to her room. It had been a long day and she was tired. She was close to finding the truth but she wasn't quite there yet. She had a feeling there was more to the story than anyone realized.

When she opened the door to her room she looked up and froze in place. Her eyes were staring at the dresser mirror. There written in red were the words, *Leave now or die in three days.*

Jillian took a deep breath and released it. She had been startled yet she should have expected something like this to happen. She took a few steps toward the mirror. Running her fingers over the letters the tips of her fingers smeared the letters. She glanced down at the dresser and found an open tube of lipstick. Someone was playing a trick on her. She called out, "Claire your little tricks aren't going to work."

Glancing around the room she didn't notice anything else out of place. The bed hadn't been disturbed and the books she had been reading were still where they should have been. Jillian walked over to the closet and opened the door. Her clothes were hanging in the same place they were earlier. Feeling more than a little foolish she even checked under the bed. When she had checked every conceivable place to hide she went back to the closet to check again for anything that shouldn't be there.

Suddenly the light in the room flickered and for a second Jillian could have sworn there was a pair of red glowing eyes stared back at her but when the lights came back on the red glowing orbs were gone. She took a deep breath and slowly closed the closet door. She went over to the bed and sat down.

The red eyes had made her want to scream but she hadn't. Those glowing eyes were just another piece of the puzzle. She had the sensation, very briefly that it hadn't been Claire standing there. But who else could it have been?

Jillian didn't even bother to get undressed. She lay back on the bed and closed her eyes. The soft light from the lamp on the table still lit the room as Jillian fell asleep.

A black aura manifested from the closet and there were two red glowing eyes staring down at her for a moment, before the aura moved toward the door and vanished completely. Jillian shivered involuntary in her sleep as the sense of being in danger from the aura passed. Something or someone didn't want her there.

She curled up on her side and brought the covers over her head. She slept undisturbed for a little while then Jillian began tossing and turning. Her dreams were being disturbed by the sound of someone calling her name.

She frowned in her sleep as she tried to place the voice with a name. When she didn't hear it again she settled into a deeper sleep. A little bit later the voice called out her name again. Instinctively she called out the name,

"Tilly."

The voice she'd heard was not unlike Claire's voice in the way she spoke but this voice was gentler, more feminine. Jillian struggled against the interruption but the voice running through her head was insistent. It called her name again.

"Jillian, time is running out. Please hear my plea. You must stop this insanity. Go to the family plot and dig around my father's headstone. You must dig up a small pouch and keep it with you."

"Why, what does it mean?" Jillian murmured.

"I don't know but I have a feeling it's important. I don't think he would have gone to the trouble of burying it if it wasn't."

"Who buried it? Did Matthew bury the pouch?" Jillian murmured.

"No, not Matthew... I know Matthew is here with you. He must find where my bones are hidden. Please tell him to find me. It's the only way to break the curse holding all of us to this place. Tell Matthew I love him, always and forever."

"But who buried the pouch?" Jillian insisted.

"George buried the pouch. He came to us looking for a job and a place to live. We gave him shelter and a job, but there was something about the man that didn't seem right."

"What was it that didn't seem right?"

"He never talked about his family and he spoke with some kind of accent. It was a little strange. Before

long he began watching us. Everything we did he was there somewhere watching us. Claire and I thought it was odd and we began to feel uncomfortable around him. Then one day I saw George burying something in the cemetery. I didn't know what it was but I think it has to do with what's going on."

"What am I supposed to do with whatever I find?"

"I don't know, it must mean something. Please help Matthew find me."

The voice faded away and Jillian was left with nothing but a sense of urgency. She struggled to wake herself up. Jillian opened her eyes and bolted upright in bed. She glanced around the room but didn't see anything. Raising her hand to her head she wiped the sweat from her forehead. This night was getting stranger and stranger.

She didn't know if what she just went through was real or not. The message was cryptic at best and she didn't know exactly what Tilly wanted her to do. She didn't understand what a small pouch had to do with anything but Tilly had been insistent on her to retrieve it.

Jillian lay back down on the bed and tried to close her eyes. She was worn out and knew she needed her rest. She couldn't go to the family cemetery plot in the dark anyway. She would need the light to find the place. She fell into a light sleep and the next thing she knew the sun was coming up in the eastern sky.

Jillian sat up on the side of the bed and rubbed her tired eyes. Her long dark hair was tousled and her eyes burned from lack of sleep but she forced herself to get up.

Walking over to the window facing the backyard Jillian looked outside. It looked the same as it had yesterday but today there was something that hadn't been there the day before. Today she knew another piece of the puzzle and she had to find what it was. Tilly hadn't known what the pouch was all about but Jillian was about to find it.

Jillian took a few minutes to change her clothes and made her way downstairs. Neither of her guests was up yet so Jillian made coffee and while it brewed she went to the back door. Looking around the back porch she found what she needed and she walked toward the cemetery plot.

As she stepped over the short fence she went directly to the biggest headstone. Kneeling beside it she read again the words written there. "Thomas Eugene Bradbury, Beloved Husband and Father." She reached out and touched the cold stone. Her fingers skimmed the letters carved in the marble and she wondered what kind of man Thomas had been.

She searched the base of the headstone but couldn't find any recent diggings. Then she shook her head. The diggings like the rest of the story would have been eighty years old. Jillian began poking around at the base of the headstone. She worked her way around the marble base and when she was halfway around the back her hand shovel brought up a small fabric pouch. Brushing off the dirt she discovered the pouch wasn't very big and it still had its bright purple color. As she tumbled the pouch in her hands she could feel something inside. She got to her feet and shoved the bag into her pocket. She would look inside the pouch later.

Jillian brushed the dirt off her knees and began her walk back to the house. When she arrived at the back door she saw Seth sitting at the kitchen table, drinking coffee. As she came in through the door Seth looked up at her.

"Good morning." Jillian smiled.

Seth nodded but didn't say anything.

Jillian cocked her head at his rudeness. "I take it you didn't sleep too well last night." She commented.

Seth grunted but still didn't say anything. Jillian ignored him and went to the sink to wash her hands. She poured herself a cup of coffee and sat down at the table with him. Neither of them said a word for a few minutes, then Seth broke the silence by asking, "Well what's on the agenda for today, more spirits roaming the hall scaring the hell out of my uncle?"

Jillian set her cup down on the table. "Excuse me?"

Seth shook his head. "No I don't think so."

"What are you accusing me of?"

"I think you know exactly what I'm saying." Seth commented. "Ever since we arrived yesterday you've bolstered my uncle belief that he's caught up in some funky curse."

"Maybe the curse is real." Jillian suggested.

Seth shook his head. "Ever since I can remember my uncle has been alone. One time I asked him about why he never married and he told me he lost the only woman he would ever love a long time ago. He also said he was cursed and he wouldn't wish that on another woman."

"What makes you think the curse isn't real?" Jillian asked.

"Curses don't exist." Seth insisted. "Matthew may have loved and lost but he's not cursed."

"How do you explain the supernatural things that have happened since you got here yesterday?"

Seth shrugged. "I don't know, maybe they've all been my imagination."

"Why is it so hard for you to believe in this sort of thing?" Jillian wanted to know.

"Why is it so easy for you to believe it?"

Jillian thought about it for a moment and then decided to tell him the real reason she came here. "My grandmother spent her honeymoon here a long time ago. She made friends with Claire and Matilda. She got a letter from Matilda just before the fire and in that letter Matilda told my grandmother that she and Matthew were running away together to get married. She also said she hated leaving in the middle of the night because she knew her leaving would hurt Claire but she felt she had no choice. She knew Claire would be hurt either way and she wanted to lessen her sister's pain."

"What does that have to do with what's going on around here?" Seth wanted to know.

"The three people that died that night had unfinished business. Someone or something stopped them from leaving here and they all need to know what the truth is. It sounds like Tilly was held against her will, Matthew couldn't get back to her and Claire was trapped in the fire. I think if we find the truth everyone will be able to move on, even your uncle."

"Even if you don't believe in the supernatural you have to know she's right." Matthew voice spoke from behind them. Both Seth and Jillian turned to see him standing in the doorway.

"Uncle Matthew, please…" Seth began only to have Matthew shake his head.

"I know, I know, you don't believe me but what Jillian said has some merit. Something happened here that shouldn't have happened. The girls and I are caught up in something that can't be explained but it's very real." Matthew came over and sat down at the table.

Jillian looked at Matthew. "Speaking of Tilly, she came to me in a dream last night."

Matthew leaned toward her. "I know I can feel her. She's very close and she's calling for me. She knows I'm here."

Jillian nodded. "She told me to tell you that you need to find her bones before the fire comes back."

"Where do we begin?" Matthew asked.

Jillian knelt down in front of Matthew and put her hand on his knee. "Can you think of any place in the Inn where a person could be hiding? A place where no one else could hear you call out if you somehow got trapped in there?"

Matthew started to shake his head but stopped. He had to think for a moment. "There was one place. I think Tilly called it the root cellar but I never knew where it was."

"What was the cellar used for? Maybe that would give us a clue where to look." Jillian told him.

Matthew thought about it for a moment and then nodded. "I believe Tilly said that at one time the Inn had been part of old plantation. After it was destroyed in the Civil War, Thomas, that was their Daddy, rebuilt the main house and made it into a home for his family. Thomas grew up here and wanted to raise his children here. The Bradbury's have owned this land since forever. She said the old root cellar was turned into a wine cellar by her father but she never took me there. She always told me no one had been down there since their father died. Although before their father died he moved most of the wine upstairs the girls had never been in the cellar. Neither of the girls drank anything stronger than tea."

Jillian shrugged. "At least we know where to start looking."

"Where is that?" Seth asked.

"The kitchen. That's where the wives would have wanted their root cellars. They stored food in the root cellars so it would have to be close to the kitchen." Jillian smiled. When she looked at Seth's face and still saw doubt there she said, "Oh come on, this could be an adventure if you looked at it that way."

"It could also be nothing more than a wild goose chase." Seth muttered.

"We have to try at least, even if it turns out to be nothing more than a wild goose chase." Jillian told them.

Brandy lifted her head from the rug when they all stood up and Jillian shook her head. "What a lazy dog. Where were you when we were visited by the ghost?"

Brandy just cocked her head and looked at Jillian as if to say, *I was right here where I belonged.*

Jillian looked around the kitchen. She opened the pantry door and went inside. Looking around she couldn't find any kind of door that lead anywhere. She came back to the kitchen and began opening cupboards. No sign of any kind of root cellar anywhere. She even went out on the back porch looking for another door that might lead them to the cellar. She found nothing.

Then she snapped her fingers. "Wait a minute. I have a blueprint drawing of the house from the realtor. Maybe the root cellar is on there." She ran for the bedroom at the top of the stairs where the file was. When she entered the bedroom she found Claire lounging on the bed. Jillian gasped and stopped in her tracks.

"You won't find my sister you know. I can't let you." Claire told her. Her eyes snapped with anger. She had one foot higher than the other and she was tapping her foot in the air.

Jillian raised her eyebrow. "Why not?"

"Because if you do find her then I will cease to exist. My time on earth, even in this form will be over and I'm not ready to depart just yet." Claire explained.

"How so?" Jillian asked.

"If you happen to find Tilly, the curse will be broken and time here will catch up with itself." Claire told her.

"Then this place is caught up in some kind of curse." Jillian said. "What happened?"

Claire shrugged. "I don't really understand it myself but George said we're caught in a time loop.'

"Who's George?"

"Never mind who George is. I'm here to tell you I can't let you find Tilly." Claire said.

"What more do you have to do here anyway?" Jillian asked as she glanced around the room for the file. She finally spotted it on the table next to the window.

"I have to atone for my mistakes in life." Claire told her.

"Then why don't you help us find your sister." Jillian asked. "Wouldn't that atone for your mistakes?"

Claire smiled briefly. "No it wouldn't. That would only send me to a hell I don't want to see."

"What do you mean?" Jillian asked.

"My sin was Cain's sin in that we each killed our sibling. Cain killed Able out of jealously as did I. I may not have done the deed myself but I am responsible for what happened to Tilly. Our fates are linked to hell and while he doesn't mind the fire and damnation, I would." Claire explained. "As long as Tilly's body is lost I'll remain here on earth. I must relive the same hell on earth that my sins created."

"Then it's true." Jillian muttered.

"What's true?" Claire asked.

"Matthew told us that you would burn the Inn down

again tomorrow night." Jillian told her.

Claire nodded. "It's that time. Every year on the day the Inn burned down it has to burn it down again. It's part of the punishment."

"You have to relive the event that caused your death until the wrong is righted." Jillian foretold.

Claire nodded. "I'm too afraid not to." She admitted. She swung her legs over the side of the bed and stood.

"What are you afraid of?" Jillian asked as she edged closer to the table the plans were on.

"I'm afraid of the hell that's waiting for me if the wrong is ever righted." Claire admitted as she began to pace. "I would rather take the burning pain of what's coming then go somewhere I don't know. George says it's the way it has to remain."

Jillian used the moment when Claire turned her back to push the plans inside her shirt. When Claire turned around to face her Jillian told her. "I can't help you with that. Each of us must face the unknown when we depart this world. I hope that you can find your salvation one day and that you can also find your courage to face what must be faced. I don't want to die tomorrow night."

Claire nodded sadly. "I would have chased you out somehow anyway. I caused the death of one innocent man I haven't taken anyone else's life but my own and Tilly's."

"And just how are you going to do that?"

Claire shrugged. "I don't know. All I do know is that you can't be here tomorrow night."

Jillian thought for a moment then had to ask, "Do you know where Tilly's body is?"

Claire stared at her for a moment, and then shook her head. "George said it didn't matter where she was, only that she was still here." She walked to the door and turned to look at her, "By the way, George isn't happy you are here, and especially Matthew. For your own sake as well as Matthew's please leave; before you can't anymore."

Jillian ran out of the room and back to the kitchen. She knew they didn't have much time and Seth and Matthew were waiting for her.

"Where have you been? We were worried about you." Seth told her.

"I ran into Claire." Jillian explained as she opened the file and spread the blueprints out on the table.

"What did she want?" Seth asked as he began looking over the blueprints. This was something he knew about. As an engineer he could read a set of blueprints.

"She told me that she couldn't allow us to find her sister. If we found Tilly then her time here would be over and she would have to leave. She's more afraid of leaving here than she is of the burning hell she herself created when she burned the Inn to the ground. She relives that hell every year."

Matthew shook his head. "Poor Claire, it didn't have to be that way at all. If she'd only let us be happy, all of us could have lived a happy life."

"I can't find the root cellar." Seth said.

"What do you mean you can't find it?" Jillian

exclaimed. "It has to be there."

"Well it's not." Seth grabbed the plans and looked them over carefully. Then he threw them down on the table. "These are useless. They were drawn up in 1962."

"What?" Jillian whispered as she sat down in her chair. "How could that be? No one's lived here since the 1930's."

Seth picked up the plans again and looked at them. "These plans were drawn by a George Walker."

"How could that be?" Matthew asked.

"What do you mean?" Jillian asked.

"George Walker lived here when I came here in 1930. He didn't say much about himself but I thought he was from the south. He had a funny sounding accent." Matthew told them.

"Why would it be so odd if he was the one that drew the plans for the house?" Seth asked.

"George never said anything but I don't think he knew how to read." Matthew said. "And there's always the fact that he burned to death in 1931."

"Well, that would make it difficult to draw plans if you can't read and you died 30 years before the plans were drawn." Jillian commented.

"I wonder how true these plans are." Seth said.

"Why what difference would that make?" Matthew asked.

"What if George is trying to hide something?"

"Like what?" Matthew asked.

Jillian thought for a moment. "If George was living

here when Matthew came here, he would have witnessed the whole affair between Tilly and Matthew and Claire's interference."

"I always thought he cared for Claire, but she had no time for him. At least she pretended she didn't have time for him. Now that I think about it I remember seeing them together at the oddest times." Matthew nodded. "The girls let him stay here and he worked around the house. The arrangement suited them both, but I think he scared them to some extent. I know Tilly wasn't comfortable around him."

"Whatever happened to him?" Jillian asked.

Matthew shrugged. "The last thing I remember from that day was when George set my luggage out on the front porch. I thought I heard someone come up behind me and the next thing I knew I was waking up on the side of the road. I don't know for sure but when I woke up I had a heck of a headache and a bump on the back of my head. I found out I was about a mile away. I knew I had to come back. I hadn't been able to say goodbye to Tilly and I didn't want to leave things like that. By the time I got back here the Inn was already burning and I couldn't get near the building."

"George never got out before the fire started. Claire told me that. He died that night along with her." Jillian asked. She picked up the blueprints and looked them over. "But if he died in the fire, how could he have left the plans and dated them in 1962?"

"Maybe he knows where Tilly is and he doesn't want anyone to find her." Matthew said.

"Is there another set of blueprints anywhere?" Seth asked. "What about a blueprint of the original plantation?"

Jillian shrugged. "I don't know of another set. In fact I'm surprised there was a plantation here at one point. We're pretty well north to have a plantation here."

"I wonder if this plantation might have been one of the places on the escape route for the slaves." Seth commented. "If that were the case there would be a more detailed map."

Jillian was trying to think of everything she knew about the place. "It seems to me there was some mention of it being on the escape route. The plantation would ship wheat to the north. I'd forgotten about that with all that's happened. I guess I got caught up in the girls and Matthew's story." She reached for the file she'd gotten earlier and opened it. She found what she was looking for and handed it over to Seth. "Here's what the realtor gave me."

Seth looked over the papers then disappeared to his room. When he got back he had a laptop computer. After researching a little of the history of Brandenburg he looked up at them. "The history of the plantation is fascinating. I found a reference to the slave route and the transportation route. Brandenburg was an important link to the northern states. Not only was wheat shipped from here but so was cotton and corn. Military supplies were also transported to resupply the Yankee troops. Also some Confederate POW's were sent to prison camps in the north from this area."

"Does the information mention anything about the original plantation?" Jillian asked.

Seth went back to his computer screen. "As a matter of fact there is an original drawing of the plantation. Is there a library in town?"

Jillian nodded. "It's right on Main Street just past the Post Office."

Seth nodded. Reaching into his pocket he brought out a flash drive and downloaded the information he wanted. He looked at Jillian and his uncle Matthew. "I'm going to make a trip into town and see what else I can find. I should be back in an hour or so."

Jillian nodded. "I should go into town too. I need some more groceries and stuff. I wasn't exactly expecting company."

"Ok we'll all make the trip." Seth said. "But let's get going so we have some time this afternoon to start searching the place. We only have one more day before the fire."

A few minutes later they were headed to town. As they left the parking lot they missed the pair of glowing eyes watching them from a room on the second floor. The eyes turned to observe the young lady resting on the sofa. "What do you think they are looking for?"

Claire glanced over to the black cloud and shrugged. "How should I know?"

"What do you think they are looking for?" The man asked again. He had transformed from the black aura into the figure of a man.

"Jillian said she was going to try and find Tilly." Claire finally told him. She had been careful to avoid him over the years but once in a while she had to speak to him. She hadn't liked him overmuch when she was alive but now he was the only one she could talk to and sometimes the isolation got to be too much for her.

He laughed out loud. "They won't find your sister. They have no clue where to look. The only plans they have for this place are ones that don't include the lower levels."

Claire smiled. "I don't know about that. The new modern history books tell of many exciting things. This place," Claire looked around the Inn, "was mentioned in the history books. It might be possible that there are other drawings that include what this place used to be. The plantation was a busy place back in its day."

"Damn," The man's figure that stood there changed again in the black aura. "We'll see about that." The aura dissipated and Claire found herself alone again. She much preferred to be alone. She got up and walked over to the front of the Inn. Looking outside she wondered if Jillian might be the one to finally break the curse that trapped them in the Inn.

She turned away from the window and paced the room. She couldn't allow them to find her sister. Just knowing she was the one that started the fire that killed three people was enough to send her to hell and that was one place she knew she didn't want to go. Claire was afraid Jillian and her friends might succeed.

Chapter Eight

An hour or so later the car pulled up to the front door. Jillian and Seth got out. Jillian went to the back of the car and began unloading the groceries while Seth helped his uncle. Matthew looked tired.

When Seth joined Jillian in the kitchen he said, "Matthew is resting."

Jillian began fixing something to eat. In a few minutes she placed a sandwich and a salad in front of Seth and joined him at the table. While he ate he began going through all the information he'd discovered at the library.

"Did you find anything about the plantation I mentioned earlier? Jillian asked.

Seth nodded. "This area was considered greatly important in reference to resupplying the Union lines, during the Civil War. I found several references to the fact they shipped everything from cannon balls to riffles to food though here. They also shipped prisoners of war north." Seth told her while he ate.

"What about the rumors they helped the slaves escape?" Jillian asked.

Seth nodded. "The Bradbury's did that too. In fact they had a map of the secret room they would allow the slaves to stay in while they waited for the right ships to come to port." He dug through the several drawings he's found to pull one or two of them out. Spreading them out on the table Jillian peeked over to have a look.

"My goodness," she said. "The Inn doesn't look anything like that anymore." She took a few minutes to look over the drawings. The plantation had been much bigger than the Inn was.

"I know, but I'm betting they might have taken down some of the plantation but I doubt they would have dug out the foundation rooms."

Jillian frowned. "What are foundation rooms?"

Seth grinned. "I hold an engineering degree but history has always been a passion of mine. If you look very closely you can see the two maps are almost identical." He showed her where the maps were the same, then he pointed out, "I said almost the same but if you look at this map a little better you can see the differences. I think this map shows the room they would have set aside for the slaves." Seth pointed out an area that wasn't covered in the first map.

"Okay, I can see the difference but the question is how do we find how to get to the basement?" Jillian asked.

"You said it yourself; the root cellar would be assessable through the kitchen. There must have been a doorway of some kind in the kitchen." Seth reminded her.

Jillian looked around the room. She and Seth both got up from the table and began looking around the kitchen. They tapped on walls and opened doors until they came to the pantry area. There was a throw rug on the floor and when they moved it Jillian was disappointed to find a solid floor and not a trap door there. They checked the walls but they seemed solid enough, at least they didn't hear an echo they would indicated an opening behind the wall. They didn't find anything until they came to the old fashioned hutch built right into the wall space. It went from wall to wall.

Jillian tapped the wall above the hutch and frowned. There was a bit of an echo. She looked at Seth and tapped again. This time they both heard a slight echo.

"Okay I think we found the false door, but how do we get it to open?" Seth murmured. He began checking the sides and back of the hutch only to find the hutch was firmly anchored to the wall.

"It looks like that piece wasn't going to be moved." Jillian said.

'No, that's true and you can't swing it toward the wall, there wouldn't have been room." Seth admitted.

Jillian thought for a moment then asked, "But could it be swung back the other way?"

Seth looked at her. "What do you mean?"

"A door can swing either way, in or out. If you couldn't swing the door in, it must go out. Does this door swing out?" She got up and began pushing on the wall above the hutch. To no avail, the wall above the hutch was nailed tight. They both tried to push the wall out but the wall didn't budge.

They both went back to the table and sat down. Jillian poured them both a cup of coffee and Seth reached for his drawings again. He studied them for a few minutes, looking for anything that would tell him how they got down to the basement area of the old plantation.

A little while later Seth got up and went back to the pantry. He knew the answer was in that room and he had to find it. A few minutes later he popped his head in the kitchen and grinned, "I think I found the answer." He told her.

Jillian got up and joined him. "What did you find?"

Seth walked over to the hutch and pressed a button he discovered on the underside of the top. The hutch moved slightly back into the wall.

Jillian gasped.

Seth's grin deepened. "Come on, we may have to push it the rest of the way. No one has used this entrance for a long time." Jillian joined him and they managed to push the hidden door open enough to slip inside the hidden stairwell.

"Oh my…" Jillian said as she peeked down into the darkness. "It has been awhile since anyone has been down here." The walls were covered in cobwebs and they could hear mice and other rodents squiring away from the sound of their voices.

"Come on," Seth urged. "We need to find some flashlights and have a look around."

Jillian stepped back into the pantry. She brushed her hair and clothing free of the cobwebs and nodded. "Okay, I think there are some flashlights in the kitchen. I may have to hunt down some batteries."

"While you do that, I'll check on Matthew. It isn't like him to sleep this long during the day." Seth told her.

Jillian quickly found the flashlights and was looking for fresh batteries when Seth came back into the room. He seemed upset. Jillian asked, "What's wrong?"

"Matthew's not in his room."

Jillian frowned. "What do you mean he's not in his room? Is he out on the front porch?"

Seth shook his head. "No, I checked there too. I've checked the entire first floor and I can't find him anywhere. It's as if he disappeared completely."

Jillian put the flashlight down on the counter and rushed to the room she put Matthew in. She could see his empty bed. The covers were messed up as if he laid on them to rest but there were little signs of a struggle anywhere else in the room. A glass of water was on the floor and his cane was still hanging on the end of the bed.

Seth came up behind her and asked, "Where else would he be?"

Jillian shrugged. "We have to find him. We'll search every room if we have to. Did you check the bathroom?"

Seth nodded. "That was the first place I looked when I couldn't find him but the bathroom is empty."

Jillian had a sinking feeling in her stomach. She thought about Claire. "Okay, you look on the first floor and I'll look upstairs. I don't know if he could have made it up the steps but I'll look up there anyway."

Seth pointed to the cane hanging on the bed rail. "I don't think he would leave his cane behind if he was walking anywhere. Don't forget he's an old man and very frail."

Jillian looked at Seth and said, "I know." Then she turned and rushed to the stairway leading to the second floor. She wasted no time and took the steps two at a time. She opened the first door and looked inside, calling Matthew's name.

She got to her room and opened the door. She found Claire resting on her bed. Jillian closed the door behind her. "What have you done with Matthew?"

Claire glanced at her and frowned. "What do you mean what have I done with Matthew?"

"Where is he?" Jillian asked again.

"I have no idea where the man is." Claire insisted. "The last time I saw him was the other night when he first arrived."

"I don't believe you." Jillian told her.

Claire got up off the bed and walked toward her. "I don't lie, little missy. And I don't take sass from anyone. What gives you the right to treat me this way?"

"Because I think you know where Matthew is and we need to find him." Jillian told her.

"I told you I haven't seen Matthew since yesterday. I have no idea where he is, nor do I care." Claire said. "I've been up here all afternoon."

Jillian stared at her for a moment then turned toward the door. Before she could leave she turned back and asked, "Is there anyone else, spirit or otherwise in the house?"

"What do you mean?" Claire asked.

"Yesterday I could have sworn I saw something in the kitchen. It was more a shadow than anything else."

Claire paled and shook her head. "I've never seen anything like that before." She told Jillian.

Jillian stared at Claire. "Now I know you're lying to me." Jillian walked around her. "Who or what is the shadowy thing I saw yesterday?" she demanded.

Claire didn't know what to tell her. George would not be pleased if she told them about him yet she didn't feel comfortable lying to anyone. "I truly didn't know Matthew was missing. I've been avoiding him."

"But what is the shadowy thing I saw?" Jillian wanted to know.

Claire began wringing her hands and pacing. "I can't tell you." She finally told her. "He wouldn't like it."

"Who wouldn't like it and why?" Jillian asked. She paused for a moment then snapped her fingers. "Is the shadowy thing George?"

"Why would you think that?" Claire whispered.

"George was the only other person that died that night eighty years ago, other than you and Tilly that is." Jillian commented. "If you are still here, it only makes sense that George would still be here too."

Claire looked worried. "George burned to death in the fire. We couldn't get out of the Inn that night. I couldn't get to Tilly either. George wouldn't let me. While the fire burned on the first floor George kept me trapped in my room."

"What happened that night, all those years ago?"

Jillian asked.

"I can't talk about it." Claire whispered. She was wringing her hands and backing away from Jillian.

"Please tell me what happened that night. It might help us find your sister and Matthew." Jillian pleaded. Jillian reached out as if to grasp her hands but Claire was too quick.

Claire shook her head. "No I can't." Then she simply vanished.

Jillian groaned in frustration. "Claire please come back. We need your help." When she didn't reappear Jillian went back downstairs. She found Seth coming back in the front door.

"Did you find him?" Seth asked.

"No," Jillian told him. "And we might not find him either."

"What does that mean?" Seth asked.

"I spoke to Claire and apparently she isn't the only ghost we have to deal with. George Walker is still here too."

Seth stared at her for a moment then threw up his hands. "You are sick, do you know that? There are no such things as ghosts. I don't know how many times I have to tell you that."

"You can deny it if you want to, I don't care but when Matthew disappeared I was with you and there was no one else in the house. Matthew never would have wandered away without telling you or without his cane. How else do you explain his disappearance?"

Seth ran his fingers through his hair. "I don't know but I can't get my head wrapped around the idea there are ghosts in the world. It's bad enough thinking humans can be so bad to one another."

"I know but we have to hurry and find Matthew. Claire wouldn't tell me where Matthew could be and I got the impression she was afraid of George."

"What does that mean?"

Jillian shook her head. "I have no idea and I don't really want to find out. Another thing, I don't think George or Claire can leave the Inn."

"What makes you think that?"

"After eighty years they are still here. If they could go anywhere I think they would have by this time."

"That means Matthew must be within the house somewhere." Seth said. "We have to start looking right away."

"Ok, we've checked the first and second floors; the only place we haven't checked is the basement." Jillian turned and went toward the kitchen. She grabbed a flashlight and handed it to Seth. Grabbing the other one she turned to the pantry area. When they got there the hutch had been pushed back to hide the stairwell to the basement. Jillian glanced at Seth, who shrugged and went to the hidden button.

Seth tried the button and when he pushed at the hutch it didn't move. He glanced at Jillian and tried again. When it didn't move the second time, Jillian stepped up and helped him. Pushing with all their might, they managed to push the hutch a few inches.

"Damn, what's going on here?" Seth said. "It wasn't this hard to open before."

Jillian leaned against the hutch. "George didn't know we found the way below before."

"I still don't know what's going on here but I'll be damned if I'm going to let this George person or ghost get away with this." Seth vowed.

"First we have to get down the steps to see what's really there." Jillian told him.

They turned and pushed again and again until they had the hutch moved back far enough for them to slip through. Seth found an old piece of wood just beyond the door and used it to brace the door open. Then he turned and clicked his flashlight on. The light cut through the total darkness that surrounded them and showed them the steps leading down into the earth.

When they reached the bottom step they found a wooden floor, not a dirt floor. Jillian moved her flashlight around and found a modern light switch on the wall. She reached out to flip the switch and the darkness was gone as the lights came on.

"What the hell?" Seth whispered as he gazed around the room they found themselves in.

Jillian looked around the room and she could see this part of the basement was set up to hold a quantity of wine bottles. Several tables were set up and a fire place in one of the corners made the room appear cozy. Jillian snapped her fingers, "I think I know what this is. In the letter from the realtor she mentioned Thomas had a wine cellar added to the Inn."

"Then maybe there was another entrance to get down here. I don't think the hutch entrance has been used since this place was a plantation." Seth told her.

Jillian nodded. "Probably not, but at the time Thomas had the Inn Prohibition would have been around so the door from the house would have been hidden."

"So where do we start looking?" Seth asked. "I want to find my uncle."

Jillian began tapping the walls and calling out Matthew's name. Seth took the other side of the room and did the same. Jillian's tapping found a hollow sound behind some shelves for books and she called Seth over to the wall. "I think there is something here."

Seth studied the wall for a moment then began running his fingers along the shelves. He had to move some books but eventually he found the hidden button. When he clicked on the button the wall opened up and led to another room.

This room reeked of spoiled fruit and had a yeasty aroma. As soon as they walked in they could feel the temperature was about 20 degrees cooler. Jillian checked the wall just inside the door and found the light switch. Snapping on the light they found themselves in a brewery of sorts.

The walls were lined with bottles of wine neatly housed on wine racks that went from floor to ceiling. In one corner there were boxes stacked three and four high that looked like they had never been open. On the side of the boxes someone had written "wine bottles." There were a couple of tables in this room and on those tables were carboys of brewing wine. Apparently when Thomas passed away he was never able to finish this wine.

They stepped further into the room and began searching the walls for another passage but didn't find anything that shouldn't have been there. "This is ridicules," Jillian said. "There must be a way out of this room. They would have had to have a way to bring supplies in and out."

"Perhaps, but however they did it, it wasn't in this room." Seth said.

"Let's go back to the tasting room and have another look. We must have missed something. Maybe there is another way out from there." Jillian suggested.

They went back to the first room they found and began searched the walls again. This time they searched every inch of the room. Jillian moved under the steps and knocked on the walls. When she tapped the walls she found an echo. Her heart skipped a beat. She turned her head and called out, "Seth, I think I found something."

Seth joined her in the cramped space and together they knocked on the wall. There was something there that was different. Seth began running his hands along the corner seams. He pulled his hand away sharply. "Ouch." He stepped back into the light to check his fingers and found blood.

Jillian peeked over his shoulder. "What happened?"

Seth looked at her and shrugged. "My hand ran into

something sharp."

Jillian looked back into the shadows under the steps. She snapped her flashlight on and went back into the alcove. "I think you found a door."

Seth joined her. "A door? Where do you see a door?"

Jillian pointed her light into the corner and they both could see a pair of rusty hinges. Seth followed the hinges up to the ceiling and along the top of the wall. It stopped at the connection right under the steps. They could see a slight seam in the wall.

"I think you're right. There is a doorway here. We just have to figure out how to get it open."

Seth reached up and began pressing the door looking for the trip switch. When he pressed the top left just under stairway the door clicked open.

Chapter Nine

It took both of them to pull the door open enough to squeeze through the opening. The door hadn't been opened in years and like the hinges it had rusted shut. The tunnel they found on the other side was dark and dank.

The floor was a dirt floor and the walls were slimy with moss. "We must have found part of the old plantation." Jillian said as she moved her flashlight around the tunnel. "Phew. I don't think there's been any fresh air down here in years."

"Probably not. Didn't Matthew say the girls didn't drink their father's wine?" Seth commented as they pushed through the tunnel. The tunnel opened up into a larger room that had several doors. This part of the building hadn't been hooked up to electricity so they had to depend on their flashlights to light their way. Seth went to the line of doors and began opening one after another. They revealed more room beyond the openings. He got to the third door and this door was a little harder to open.

Jillian joined him and together they forced the door open. On the other side they could feel fresh air. Once they pushed it open enough to see beyond a few feet Jillian noticed brush and undergrowth was blocking the entrance.

The fresh air felt good on her skin. Jillian turned her back to the door and dug in her feet. Pushing with everything she had inside her the door suddenly gave way and they both tumbled outside.

Jillian ended up on top of Seth. "Oh my gosh, I'm so sorry."

Seth grinned. "Not a problem sweetheart."

Jillian flushed and stood up. Looking around she could see they were in the back yard. Brushing the cobwebs and dirt from her clothes she commented. "I haven't had a chance to discover the secrets of the back yard yet." She glanced at the opening of the door. "And I doubt I would have discovered the door with all this brush in front of it."

Seth was standing and as he brushed his clothes off he looked around. "Well it makes sense that it's located here."

Jillian stared at him. "Why would its location be so obvious?"

Seth pointed to the back door of the Inn. "I saw a picture of the plantation at the library this afternoon. The Inn is the main part of the plantation, attached to the main part would be the slave quarters and storage areas. Those areas are gone now but they would have had underground storage to keep their produce cool in the fall and not frozen in the winter."

"Okay I can understand that but it doesn't really help us find your uncle." Jillian said.

Seth looked back at the cellar. "I know but now that we have the door open there will be a little more light. Come on, let's have a look around."

Jillian followed him back underground. Dust swirled in the daylight coming through the door. This room was very large with several rooms leading off the main one.

"This is as good as any place to start looking for your uncle." Jillian stated.

Seth went over to the first door and tried to open it. Jillian went over to the other side and began opening the doors. She got the first one open but there was nothing inside. She went to the second door and was reaching for the handle when a sound from inside caught her attention. She glanced over at Seth and motioned for him to come over to her.

Seth approached the door and pressed his ears to the wooden panel. When he heard the sound he backed up and pounded on the door. "Uncle Matthew, are you in there?"

There was more noise from the room and Seth reached for the door. The handle broke off in his hand when he tried to turn in and Seth swore. He pounded on the door and said, "We're working on getting you out, Uncle Matthew, but it's going to take a little while. The handle broke off."

Seth looked around the room for something to help open the door. Jillian saw something that might help and she walked over to the table almost hidden in the dark. She found a hammer. Her eye caught the sight of something oddly out of place. Sitting there on the table was ladies hanky. It was dingy from being left on the table for all these years but the embroidery work could still be seen. Jillian grabbed it and pushed it down into hcr pocket and grabbed the hammer. She also picked up what looked like a chisel. Walking back over to the door she handed the tools to Seth.

Seth went to work on the hinges. Tapping the chisel on the hinge pins he worked one then the other. Jillian kept her flashlight on the hinges as Seth worked them. When the second pin was out Seth flung the tools down on the floor and kicked the door away from the hinges.

Jillian shined her light around the room and found Matthew curled up in the corner. His clothes were dusty but he seemed alert. Seth rushed over to him and helped him to his feet. Jillian waited until they got closer to slip her arm around the other side of Matthew. They led him out of the main room through the door to the back yard.

Matthew shielded his eyes against the bright sunlight. He stumbled on the uneven ground. Seth and Jillian tightened their hold on him and in a few minutes they got him to the kitchen. Seth led his uncle to a chair while Jillian went to get a wet cloth.

When she couldn't find one handy enough she remembered the hanky she found earlier. She took it out of her pocket and began rinsing it. Warm water rinsed most of the dirt and grime out of the material. As she squeezed the water out of the hanky she found the embroidery work looked very good. She examined it closer and found the work looked almost professional. She rinsed it again and brought it over to Matthew. She handed it to him and watched as he ran the material over his face. His hands shook as he removed the dust and dirt from his face.

Jillian turned away to get him a drink of water when Matthew groaned. She turned back to see him staring at the hanky in his hand.

Matthew looked up at her and asked, "Where did you find this?" He shook out the small scrap of material to view the M embroidered in the corner of the cloth.

Jillian glanced at Seth then back at Matthew. "I found it in the main room we rescued you from, why?"

Matthew looked back at the cloth. "This was Tilly's favorite hanky. She loved the flowers, roses were her favorite." Matthew's fingers went to the single rose embroidered next to the M. "She loved the color of the Tiffany rose. She said it reminded her of the early dawn as the sun came over the top of the bluffs."

Jillian came and knelt beside Matthew. "Are you okay? Do you remember how you got down there? In the basement I mean."

Matthew shook his head. "The last thing I remember is laying down to rest. At my age I need a lot of rest. Anyway I lay down on the bed and I was almost asleep when I heard a sound. I tried to open my eyes but all I saw was blackness. I felt something heavy on my body and then I found myself alone in the dark, down in that room." He paused to take a drink of water then continued, "I tried to call out but I couldn't."

Seth knelt beside his uncle. "We found you Uncle Matthew."

Matthew turned to his nephew and patted his hand. "I knew you would but it was so dark down there. I was afraid you wouldn't find me in time. The longer I was in that room the colder I got." Matthew hesitated for a moment and said, "But I didn't feel like I was alone somehow." He looked down at the hanky in his hand. Looking up at Jillian he asked, "Where did you say you found this?"

Jillian glanced at Matthew, "I found it on the table in the main room. I don't even know what made me pick it up."

Matthew struggled to get to his feet. When he was standing he told them, "We have to go back to that room. That must be where Tilly is. She must be in one of the other rooms down there."

"Matthew," Jillian cautioned. "You must rest, at least until you get your strength back."

Matthew smiled at her and said, "My dear, I'll have all of eternity to sleep after I die, right now I need to find my Tilly."

Jillian glanced over at Seth and saw him shrug. "Okay, we can go back down there, but this time we take caution. There is something or someone here that doesn't want us to find Tilly."

A few minutes later the three of them set out for the basement.

Chapter Ten

When they reached the entrance Seth led the way inside. The darkness wasn't as black this time as daylight tried to reach into the room from the open door. Seth found a stool in a corner of the room and placed it in the middle so Matthew could sit down.

"But I don't want to sit down. I want to find Tilly." Matthew argued about sitting out the hunt but Seth was adamant.

"Uncle Matthew, you need to rest." Seth told him. "Jillian and I can search for her, but you need to rest."

Matthew growled but he sat down. He could feel something in the air. It felt like part excitement part dread, and he didn't know which part he was rooting for. He could almost feel Tilly was nearby, yet part of him was hoping she wasn't.

He knew deep down in his heart she had been dead all these years, and for that his heart ached, but he knew he had to find where her bones were hidden. He knew if he did he would free her spirit. He couldn't wait to see her again. He was almost giddy with feeling he hadn't felt for eighty years.

He had been waiting for her for so long. When he got back to the Inn that night so long ago he knew something held him back. Some force other than nature prevented him from getting close to the Inn that night. He hadn't thought about it until now.

He closed his eyes and tipped his head back. He concentrated on Tilly. He smiled as he recalled her face in the sunlight. He thought back to a happier time when they were together. Matthew was remembering the picnic they had. That was the day Matthew finally told Tilly he had fallen in love with her.

The day had been a warm late autumn day. They had gone on a picnic and full of fried chicken and coleslaw, Matthew had lifted his glass of wine and toasted her.

"Here's to the most beautiful woman in my world."

Tilly had blushed. "You are such a rascal. You know you don't mean that at all. I'm sure the other women in your life are more beautiful than I am."

Matthew shook his head. "All I can see is your beauty. Woman, you have spoiled me for any other female on earth." He hesitated then continued. "Don't you know that the sun and moon reflect your moods? Maybe that's fanciful thinking but you are the most important single thing in my life?"

Tilly took her hanky and covered her face. "Matthew, you're making me blush with all your crazy talk."

Matthew reached over and lowered her hands from her face. He could see her flushed cheeks and the love she had for him in her eyes. "Don't you know that I love you? Can't you feel it every time I look at you? I want to spend the rest of my life with you. I want to give you everything you desire and call you my wife."

He watched as Tilly fully realized what he meant. He waited with open arms as she came to him and sealed their love with a kiss so full of passion it threatened to blot out the sun.

Matthew came back to this world with a thud as Seth pounded on the door closest to him. Matthew watched as Seth and Jillian broke into the room. He struggled to get to his feet and wandered to the open doorway. The room was empty but showed Matthew what a desolate forgotten space this was.

He turned to go back to his seat when he felt a breeze over his face. It smelled like lavender and roses. The scent reminded him of Tilly. "Tilly." He whispered. His body felt weak for a moment and he leaned against the wall for support.

Another slight breeze carried her voice to him. "Matthew, you're here."

Matthew closed his eyes and whispered, "I'm here to find you and I won't stop until I do. I love you Tilly."

"I'm here Matthew. I'm right here, waiting for you." Matthew heard Tilly say. "Please hurry before he comes back."

"Before who comes back?" Matthew asked.

"George carried me down to this hell hole a long time ago. He locked me in this room and walked away. I cried to him for mercy, for him to let me out but he told he couldn't allow you and me to be together."

"What does that have to do with you being down here?"

"George told me he had created a loop hole. He said he would have all the time in the world but he needed us out of the way."

"What are you talking about?" Matthew asked out loud. He hadn't realized the conversation was taking place in his mind.

"Matthew, are you all right?" Jillian asked as she moved closer to him. She led him back to his chair and when he was seated she knelt beside him. "What is it?"

Matthew glanced down at her and said, "Tilly is down here. George brought her down here just before the fire. He locked her in one of the room and just left her."

Jillian glanced at Seth then back to Matthew. "How do you know that?"

Matthew shook his head. "She told me. She's very close to us and she called out to me. I know you don't believe me but she did."

Jillian patted Matthew's knee. "Matthew, I do believe you. I think you and Tilly need each other more than you realize. What else did Tilly tell you?"

"She said George told her he created some kind of loop hole. He told her with us out of the way he would have all the time he needed."

"What would he need time for?" Jillian asked.

Matthew shook his head. "She didn't say." Matthew's eyes filled with tears. "What could she have ever done to George to warrant this treatment? Tilly was the gentlest soul I ever knew."

Jillian patted his knee. "I don't think it was anything

Tilly did. I think it was something Claire did."

Matthew frowned. "What do you mean something Claire did? Claire might have been a pain in the butt at times but she couldn't hurt anyone, well not really."

"Think about it for a moment," Jillian told him. "I think Claire lusted after you and she didn't want Tilly to get you. She went out of her way to put road blocks up so Tilly wouldn't run away with you."

Matthew shook his head. "But she wasn't a bad person. She was just jealous. She thought she wanted me but I only had eyes for Tilly. I kept trying to tell Claire that I couldn't love her in the way she wanted. That last day she tricked us and it nearly broke us apart forever but I came back for Tilly. I just came back too late."

"We'll find her, I promise." Jillian told him.

Matthew patted her hand. "I know we will. I can feel it in my bones. Maybe once we do we can end this curse."

Jillian thought for a moment then added, "Matthew, you do realize that if we end the curse, you might die, don't you?"

Matthew smiled. "Yes I realize that, my dear. That is exactly what I hope will happen. I know that I was never meant to live this long. We have to right the wrong that's being played out here. The night of the fire three people died but some kind of magic is keeping everyone alive long after their time on earth was up."

They were interrupted by Seth opening yet another room in the basement. This one too was empty. Seth looked back at Matthew and Jillian and shook his head. He moved on to the last room on the right side. He tried the door handle first but it wouldn't budge. He grabbed the hammer and chisel to remove the hinges.

With the first bang he heard something he didn't with all the others. He thought he heard someone calling his name. He dropped the hammer and backed away from the door. He quickly glanced at Matthew and Jillian then back to the door. "What the hell?" Seth whispered.

Matthew struggled to his feet and moved closer to the door. "Tilly, are you in there?" he whispered.

There was some movement behind the door. Someone banged on the door from the other side and all three could hear a female voice call out, "Matthew, is that you? Please help me get out of here."

Seth bent over to pick up the hammer. He began tapping the hinges, first one then the other. The door slid out of its opening slightly. Seth and Jillian moved the door completely out of its opening and when Jillian shined her flashlight in the dark they all found Tilly's final resting place. Matthew stumbled back and came to rest against the table in the corner. He whispered, "Tilly."

Seth and Jillian watched as something stirred in the corner. A ghostly spirit rose and began walking toward Matthew. She stopped when she got close to him. She reached out her hands and he took them in his. "Oh Matthew, I have waited for this day for so long."

"Tilly, I have missed you girl." Matthew's tears spilled out and down his face.

Tilly turned to look at Jillian and Seth. "I thank you for finding me after all this time." She looked back to Matthew and said, "And for bringing my Matthew back to me."

"What happens now?" Matthew asked. "How do I join you?"

"NO!" they all heard someone shout. "This will not happen." Everyone turned to the door to find a black aura blocking out the light.

Matthew stood up and moved to stand between the black aura and Tilly. "I don't know who you are but you aren't going to get Tilly again."

The black aura throbbed with rage and everyone could feel it pulsating in the small room. "This time I shall enjoy killing you old man. I should have done it eighty years ago." The black aura reached out and took Matthew by the throat. Invisible hands lifted Matthew up off the floor and threw Matthew's body across the room. Matthew's body was lifted again this time almost to the ceiling and dropped to the floor again.

Tilly screamed at the sight of Matthew's crumpled body.

"Uncle Matthew," Seth called out as he rushed to his uncle's body. He felt for a pulse but didn't find one.

Jillian looked at Tilly as she knelt beside Matthew's body. "Oh Matthew, I am so sorry." Tilly wept.

Matthew's body shimmered for a moment then his ghost rose up and he took her hand. As she stood beside him, Matthew told her, "Don't be sorry. Now I'm free to join you." Matthew raised one of Tilly's hands to his lips. Kissing her fingers he told her, "But we can't leave just yet. We have to stop George from continuing this loop forever."

Matthew glanced down at his mortal body and then he looked at Seth. "Don't be sorry about my death. I lived a long life but now I'm back with the woman I love."

Tilly turned to look at Jillian. "Did you find the small pouch I told you about?"

"Do you know what the pouch means?" Jillian asked as she fished it out of her pocket.

Tilly looked at Matthew. "No I don't but I don't think George is really who he claims to be."

"What are you talking about?" Matthew asked.

"I don't think George is who he says he is." Tilly repeated. "I think he's from the Deep South, New Orleans perhaps."

"What makes you think that and what does it have to do with this situation?" Seth asked.

Tilly raised her hand, "Please bear with me. I know this may sound strange but back in my day, it wasn't so strange. I found a letter once in George's room when I was cleaning. It looked like an old letter but it wasn't addressed to George Walker, it was addressed to Beau Lamprey." She began to pace. "I didn't read the letter as it was none of my business but after I found it I began to notice some things that were happening. Shortly after that I noticed a favorite ring of mine disappeared. I asked Claire about it but she hadn't touched it. Then she told me one of her favorite combs was missing."

Matthew raised his head. "Was that around the time I asked about my pin?" He looked over at Seth and told him, "When I got out of the military I was given a pin of the flag. I always wore in on my lapel and one day it just disappeared."

"That was about the time I saw George digging around my father's headstone. I don't know what he buried that day but when he finished he looked around almost as if he expected someone to catch him doing something wrong." Tilly said. "That was three days before the fire."

Jillian thought for a moment then reached inside her pocket. "I found this buried by your father's headstone. I don't know what it means but the bag looks almost brand new."

Tilly looked at the bag and looked at Jillian. "Can you open it?"

Jillian opened the bag and spilled the contents out in her hand. There was a ladies ring, a hair comb, a small pin and a key ring. There was also a dried up chicken's foot and various dried herbs. The personal items were coated in what looked like dried blood.

Jillian looked at the items in her hand and frowned. "What the heck is all this stuff and what does it mean?"

Tilly gasped and backed away. "It's voodoo, that's what it is."

Jillian glanced at Seth and back to Tilly. "Voodoo? Don't tell me you actually believe in that crap?"

Tilly stared at her for a moment and nodded. "Back in my day voodoo existed and even if you didn't believe it was very real. My friends told me about it. They traveled down to New Orleans once and they saw it. It was everywhere down there and the stories they told me frightened me."

"What sort of things did they tell you?" Matthew asked.

"Voodoo was everywhere and down there it was a big thing. People used it to put a curse on someone they didn't like or it could be used as a love potion, or to help someone who was sick." Tilly shook her head. "I don't know how it worked but my friend Eleanor swears it works."

"Could this be what's held you and the Inn in limbo all these years?" Jillian asked.

"I don't know, maybe." Tilly said. "What difference does it make?"

Jillian put the items back into the bag. "It makes a difference because for the first time in eighty years the bag isn't buried anymore. Whatever time loop George put on the Inn isn't in place this year. If the fire consumes the Inn again, this time it may be real."

Chapter Eleven

Jillian glanced over at Matthew's mortal body. "We need to get the police out here to take care of Matthew's body. George can't do anything until tomorrow. Right now he doesn't know we have the pouch. We have until tomorrow to find a way around the fire."

"There is one more thing we have to do before the fire." Tilly stated.

"What would that be?" Jillian asked.

"I need to talk to Claire. I want her to know that I forgive her for her part of what happened to me."

Matthew hugged her then looked in her eyes. "Can you really do that? Forgive her I mean? She brought us so much trouble."

Tilly raised her hands and placed them on either side of his face. "My darling, I know Claire has done many things wrong in her life, I won't say that she hasn't, but she isn't malicious. She just doesn't think things through all the way." She glanced over at Jillian. "Part of what's kept this loop going is the fact that Claire feels responsible for this mess. She feels guilty that she allowed George to take over. She has to know that I can forgive her."

"I don't know why that would be important to you; after all, she did contribute to your death." Seth told them.

"Because I could never hope to move on with Matthew until I tell Claire I forgive her." Tilly said. "I won't have this hanging over our heads the rest of eternity."

"Claire will be at peace then too." Jillian said. "I know she regrets the events of the past that led to this. She said earlier that she wishes she could go back and do things differently."

"Ok, let's just get this over with. We have to contact the police. What are we going to tell them about how Matthew died?" Seth asked.

Jillian reached out and placed her hand over Seth's. "Matthew was over a hundred years old. I don't think it would be wrong to say he died in his sleep."

"If anything the town's people are going to be too afraid to ask too many questions." Matthew offered his opinion. "They know as well as we do the anniversary of the fire that destroyed this place is only one day away."

"We'll have to carry his body upstairs." Seth said. Jillian moved over to his feet and when Seth lifted his uncle's shoulders up off the floor Jillian lifted his feet. They moved toward the door and out into the back yard. Making their way through the kitchen and dining room they finally came to Matthew's bedroom. Carefully laying his body on the bed, Seth and Jillian took a step back. Matthew looked as if he was resting but they knew he wasn't.

Seth went to take off his uncle's shoes and he pulled the blanket up around Matthew's waist. "I don't know if they'll believe it or not." He told Jillian.

"They may not look that closely." Jillian offered. "Come on we have to find Claire."

Seth and Jillian went back to the kitchen. They found Tilly and Matthew waiting for them. Tilly was glancing around the kitchen nervously.

"What's wrong?" Jillian asked.

Tilly shrugged. "I don't know. I feel something but I can't put my finger on what's wrong."

Suddenly there was an unearthly scream of fury and Jillian turned to face the steps. Claire stood at the doorway and stared at the sight of Matthew and her sister Matilda. Her hands went to her mouth as she cried out in anguish, "No, you can't be together."

"But we are." Matthew's arms encircled Tilly and they both looked at Claire. "Matthew came back for me even after all these years."

"How did you find her?" Claire whispered. "I've been looking for her final resting place for a long time and I could never find it."

"Why were you looking for me?" Tilly asked.

Claire wiped tears from her face. Wringing her hands she told them, "I realized my mistake when I saw the devastation on your face when you came in and found me with Matthew. I wanted to run to you and explain what I did but after I got dressed, I couldn't find you."

"When I left my room I ran into George. He could tell I was crying and when he asked me what happened I'm afraid I blurted out the truth." Tilly admitted. "He looked crushed, and then he looked angry. He grabbed my arm and hauled me outside. He demanded that I tell him exactly what I saw in detail and when I did he grew very upset. He started saying something about being betrayed."

Tilly glanced at her sister and said, "I think he loved you Claire and he saw this act as a betrayal he couldn't forgive. He grabbed me again and forced me into the basement. He locked me in that room but before he closed the door he told me he was going to fix you. He was going to going to fix things so he would have all the time he needed to make you see that you loved him." Tilly shivered. "He was crazy that night. When he closed the door I heard him lock it, then I didn't hear anything. I banged on the door and I screamed but no one came."

"I never knew what happened to you." Claire admitted. "As soon as I could I looked for you. Matthew had left already and the only person I could find was George. He told me he hadn't seen you. I had no reason not to believe him. It was about an hour later he rushed upstairs to find me. He told me the Inn was on fire and we would have to hurry if we wanted to get out."

"Did he tell you what started the fire?" Seth asked.

"He told me my dog Sammy knocked over a lamp. We always had oil lamps in the parlor and he said Sammy knocked one over chasing a squirrel. When we came down the stairs the fire was everywhere. We couldn't get out. We rushed back upstairs and tried to get out the backstairs but they were blocked too." Claire paused as she remembered the last few minutes of her mortal life. "I was so afraid as the smoke got closer. George stayed with me the whole time. When the smoke got closer he asked me if I was afraid to die. When I told him yes, he asked me what I wanted him to do. I told him to save me and then he began to chant something. I didn't understand it but he kept chanting. Then everything went black. I couldn't see anything or feel anything. I knew for at least a little while I was alone. Then I felt the cold. It hurt to breath and I felt someone grabbing my arms and he pulled me toward him. I was so grateful I allowed him to take care of me." Claire shook her head. "It wasn't until much later that I began to ask questions.

"What happened then?" Tilly asked.

Claire looked at her sister. "That's when he told me what happened the night of the fire. He said we both died that night. I couldn't believe it. I didn't feel any different yet I knew I was. George told me everything would be okay but we couldn't leave the Inn. He told me we would live forever as long as no one found your resting place. If you were found we would both go to hell as punishment. He said he invoked some old magic he'd learned from his grandmother. I was so afraid I didn't ask him about that."

"Did he say what would happen now?" Jillian wanted to know.

Claire shook her head. "George hasn't been happy the last few days. He knows Matthew is here and he's not very happy. Oh Tilly, he scares me when he's like this."

"He must be able to move around the Inn. He took Matthew from his room to the basement. He left him down near the same place he put Tilly." Jillian told Claire. "Do you know how he did that?"

Claire shook her head. "Right after the fire he tried to tell me that he loved me but I told him I never thought about him that way. I told him there was something in his past I couldn't understand. He asked what it was and I told him I read a letter I found in his room. At first he was angry that I would snoop through his things. The letter was addressed to Beau Lamprey. The letter told him he couldn't ever come back home. The police were looking for him and they wouldn't understand why he had to do what he did."

"Did the letter say what Beau did?" Jillian asked.

Claire shook her head. "I asked him about it but he wouldn't tell me. He told me the man in that letter died a long time ago. He said he left Beau Lamprey in New Orleans and when he came north he became George Walker."

Jillian glanced at the windows and noticed for the first time it was dark outside. She was surprised at the passing of so much time. She glanced at the clock and noticed it was seven thirty. "We don't have much time left." She told Seth.

Claire turned to look at the window. She became very nervous. She looked at her sister and said, "I am so sorry I tricked you with Matthew. I felt you were pulling away from me and I didn't want to be left here alone. It never occurred to me that you might really love him, not until I saw your face when you found us in bed together."

Tilly walked over to her sister. "I know. It was very difficult for me too. I didn't want to leave you but I was so much in love with Matthew I didn't care about anything else. Down in that room I had a lot of time to think about things."

"What do you mean you had a long time to think about things?" Claire asked. "I thought the fire killed you?"

"No, it wasn't the fire that ended my life. I didn't know about the fire. I was left alone in the dark with no food or water. I figure I lasted about two weeks before I gave up."

Claire raised both hands to her mouth. "No," she whispered. "I didn't know where you were, I swear. I am so sorry."

Tilly smiled at her sister and took her into her arms. "I know, my darling. This wasn't your fault. I know you would have come to me if you could have. I understand that now, and I can forgive you for your part in all of this."

Claire stared at her sister for the longest time before she asked, "How can you forgive me?"

Tilly smiled. "Because I love you, you goose. You are my sister and I love you dearly."

Claire turned her head to Matthew. "Can you forgive me too?"

"I can if it frees your soul. I came back here for five years to try and figure out what happened that night. I didn't come back because it was too hard to watch the fire burn down everything I loved every year, knowing I couldn't stop it from happening." Matthew told her.

"Now that you and Matthew are back together and you have forgiven me I suppose I'll have to face whatever fate has given me." Claire finally said.

"Wait a minute," Jillian finally realized something. "Why haven't you and Matthew moved on yet?"

"What are you talking about?" Seth asked.

Jillian shrugged. "I just thought once their unfinished business was finished they would move on to the ghostly plane or wherever ghosts go. No one has moved on yet."

Suddenly the lights in the kitchen went out and the room was plunged into darkness. Claire screamed. For a few minutes no one said a word. Then the lights came back on but they could all see the room had one more presence in it. A black cloud shimmered near the back door and they could all feel the rage pulsing from it.

"George." Claire whispered.

Chapter Twelve

The black cloud took the shape of a man. His features were badly burned from the fire eighty years ago. His face looked almost demonic as his rage spilled over. "No one is going anywhere. I saw to that eighty years ago."

Claire moved to stand with Tilly and Matthew. Seth and Jillian stood their ground. "What is that supposed to mean?" Seth asked.

"The four of us will never leave these walls. Ever year the Inn burns to the ground and every year it comes back from the flames of hell as if nothing has touched it. It's been happening for eighty year and it will happen again for the next eighty years." George told them. Then he looked at Seth and Jillian. "This year you will join us in the hell of burning to death but unlike us you will not be back. Your souls will be lost forever. You should have left when I told you to go. Now it's too late for you."

Jillian frowned. "You are the one that wrote the messages, aren't you?"

"What messages?" Seth asked.

"The first night I was here I found a message written in dust on the table and then I found one written in lipstick on the mirror in my bedroom. I thought the warnings were from Claire."

George sneered. "Yes, I wrote the warnings but you were too stupid to listen to them, now the fire will take your life too."

"But the fire doesn't start until tomorrow." Jillian argued.

George shook his head. "None of you are leaving this Inn. No one can leave and no one else can get in."

"George you can't let them die." Tilly said. "That would be murder."

George looked her in the eye and said, "It wouldn't be the first murder I've committed." He turned his head to stare at Claire. "Just ask Claire. Ask her about a certain letter she read a long time ago."

"But you never told me what the letter meant." Claire cried out. "I didn't read the whole letter, only the first few paragraphs."

"Then I guess we're all going to hell, aren't we?" George said.

"What did the letter say?" Jillian asked. "I think we all have a right to know."

"What rights do you all have to know my business?" George's rage spilled out. "What rights do you think you have regarding me?"

"If we're all going to die I think we have the right to know why?" Jillian said.

"The letter meant I could never go home again." George screamed at them. "My grandmother told me I could never come back to the bayou I was raised on. I could never again feel the warm waters I swam in as a boy. Never again would I smell the smoke of a sycamore tree as it cooked the food of my native home."

"Why couldn't you go back?" Jillian asked.

George turned his head and glared at her. "Because I took the life of a man that was beating my mother to death. He thought he caught her cheating on him again and this was the last straw. According to tradition he began beating her in front of the family she wronged and they all stood there and let him do it. When I couldn't bear her screams anymore I tried to stop him but I couldn't. He was too caught up in the moment and before I knew it I had my knife in my hand and I had plunged it into his chest."

"What happened then?" Jillian asked.

"My grandfather walked over to my father and took my knife out of his chest and he put a streak of my father's blood on my forehead. Then he and my three uncles took my father's body away and everyone disappeared. I was left there alone with my mother. When I went to check on her she was dead. My father's beating had killed her." George reached up to his forehead and searched for the streak of blood that stained his soul. The blood wasn't there but he felt it all the same. "I left the bayou that night and I haven't ever been back."

"Surely your family has forgiven you by this time." Seth reasoned.

George looked at him and shook his head. "No they haven't and they never will. Bayou people are set in their ways and ain't nobody going to change them." George slipped into his native dialect.

"Why did you stop your father that night?" Jillian asked.

George turned his head to look at her. "Nobody ever asked me that before." He paused and then told them, "My mother never cheated on my father. My father was nothing more than a jealous fool. He had a mean streak in him a mile wide but she loved him. When he had a little drink in him he got mean and that night he had more than a little drink in him. Earlier that day we caught us a gator in the swamps and we were celebrating the catch, when he started in on my mother."

He paused and told them, "What happened in the past stays in the past, nothing can be done about it."

"But the past doesn't have to keep repeating itself." Jillian argued. "The circumstances of that night eighty years ago have changed. We found where you hid Tilly and she and Matthew are together again. Tilly has forgiven her sister."

George shook his head. "That doesn't matter anymore. I put a curse on the Inn and all the people in it. The fire will happen again and this time your souls will join ours."

"What would happen if the curse wasn't a factor anymore?" Jillian asked as she dug in her pocket.

"What do you mean by that?" George asked. "No one can stop a curse."

Jillian held out the small purple pouch she'd dug up. When George saw it he slowly backed away with a look of horror on his face.

He looked up at Jillian. "You crazy woman, you can't remove a curse by digging up the bag. All you did was make sure this time we will all go the hell." He began to dissipate into his black cloud form and from that he disappeared altogether.

Seth walked over to the back door and tried the handle. As George told them the door was sealed shut. Seth disappeared for a few minutes and when he came back he said, "We can't get out either door. The front door is sealed too."

"What about the door we found downstairs?" Jillian suggested. "Maybe he missed that one."

"I can try it but I don't think he would have overlooked any escape route." Seth told them. He took a flashlight with him and went to the pantry. He was gone for quite a while and when he returned he shook his head. "The door is shut tight. I couldn't even get the hinges loose."

Jillian sat down on a chair. She glanced at the clock and noted the time. "Then we have less than twenty four hours to live. When he starts the fire again we're all going to die again."

"Wait a minute, what did you say?" Matthew asked.

Jillian looked at him. "What did I say?"

"You said when he starts the fire," Matthew repeated. "How do you know it was George that started the fire?"

"George always told me my dog tipped over a lamp in the parlor." Claire stated.

Jillian shrugged. "At this point does it really matter who started the fire?"

Matthew sat down at the table with Jillian. "I know

this may sound strange but when the Inn reappeared all those years ago and kept reappearing I did some research. I couldn't find much out, back then voodoo wasn't something people talked about. It wasn't until recently that anybody knew anything about it."

"Uncle Matthew, what did you find out?" Seth asked his uncle. He knew from growing up around Matthew that he could get sidetracked easily.

Matthew glared at him and continued his story, "I found out that if a time loop is started by a fire and the loop is interrupted the fire will happen one last time and it will destroy everything as it did the first time."

"Isn't that what George said?" Jillian asked.

"But things are different this time." Matthew said. "This time you and Seth are here and you have his pouch."

"I don't think my having the pouch is going to save us."

"True but this time the fire will not be stopped. This time we won't wake up tomorrow morning, like we've done for the last eighty years." Matthew said.

"If your dog started the fire where is her body?" Jillian asked.

Claire shrugged. "I haven't seen the dog since the fire began. When I asked George about where the dog was he told me she must have died outside."

"I remember when I tried to get close to the front door I tripped over something. I think it was Sammy's body. She was out in the yard." Matthew told them. "When the sun came up the next morning I saw her body and

Sammy was dead but there wasn't a singed hair on her head. It looked to me like her neck had been broken." Matthew shook his head. "I buried her under the big oak tree in the front yard."

"What if it wasn't your dog that started the fire at all? What if George started the fire." Jillian asked.

"Why would he do that?" Tilly asked.

"For the same reason he took you to the basement." Jillian told them.

"Do you know something the rest of us don't?" Seth asked.

"I think George has been in love with Claire all this time." Jillian concluded.

"Me? He was in love with me?" Claire was astounded. "But I told him a long time ago I never thought about him in that way."

Jillian nodded. "I know you did but he loved you all the same."

"How do you know this?" Seth asked.

"It all makes sense." Jillian pointed out. "He said he did all of this for you. What if, like his father he's nothing more than a jealous fool? What if he took Tilly to the basement because he thought she was in your way? What if he cursed this place to give himself time to get you to fall in love with him?"

"That's a lot of what ifs." Seth stated.

Claire thought for a moment. "You know what; I think you're on to something there. The first few years he was here he was sweet on me I think." She shuddered briefly, and then said, "But I never thought about him that way. He scares me too much. There is a very dark side to him."

"Was there ever a time he tried to tell you about his feelings and you brushed him aside?" Jillian wanted to know.

Claire thought back for a moment then nodded her head, "It was about a week before the fire. Tilly and Matthew were having a picnic and George came to me. He said something about being alone and did I want to go on a picnic with him. When I told him no he looked crushed for a moment. I didn't think about it anymore after that. I wasn't thinking about anything after that except for getting Matthew for myself. I didn't realize my actions would come back and bite me in the butt so badly." Claire began wringing her hands together. "All of this is my fault and I deserve it but you all don't. I'm so sorry this happened." Tears rolled down her cheeks and she ran from the room.

"Oh dear, I didn't mean to make her cry." Jillian looked at Tilly.

"Don't worry about it. Claire always had the flare for drama. Maybe I can talk to her." Tilly walked out of the kitchen to look for her sister.

Jillian looked at Seth. "Can you use your computer to find out something about voodoo curses and time loops? Maybe the world has discovered something we can use to break the curse."

Matthew came over to where Jillian sat and sat down next to her. He reached out and patted her hands. "I hope you can find a way out of this damnedable curse. You and Seth don't deserve this."

Jillian looked at him and smiled. "You didn't deserve it either."

"But maybe I did." Matthew said quietly.

"What do you mean?"

"I came here a broken man." Matthew said. "I couldn't get over what I was forced to do in the War. I hated killing the men I killed. My soul hurt deep down inside me. I carried their faces with me everywhere I went. Their screams haunted me every time I closed my eyes. Then I came here, and this place offered me a solace I never thought I would find again. Walking these hills I found a peace I didn't know if I deserved or not. I had done some terrible things but the hills accepted my pain and released it from my soul. I could breathe again without the hurt stabbing my lungs."

"What happened then?" Jillian asked.

"When I was myself again I noticed Tilly. She was such an angel. She was soft where a woman should be soft, tough when she needed to be and she was very understanding. I couldn't help but fall in love with her. Suddenly she became my reason for living."

"Then Claire threw a monkey wrench into the mix." Jillian added.

"Then Claire threw a monkey wrench into the mix," Matthew repeated. "Tilly and I had decided to elope and we were going to leave that very night. The next thing I knew I was waking up in bed with Claire and when I saw the look of betrayal on Tilly's face I think I died a little that day."

"What happened after that?"

"I was so mad at Claire I knew if I didn't leave I thought I would kill her. In one swift moment of time, she had taken everything I had and turned it to dust. I left a broken man. Claire told me to leave and I was on my way out the door when someone hit me from behind. When I came too that night I made up my mind I was going to get my Tilly back. I hadn't done anything wrong. I don't know how Claire managed to get me into her bed but I hadn't done anything wrong. Well," he said. "You know the rest. By the time I got back here the Inn was burning and all I could hear was their screams of terror."

Tilly came to the door of the kitchen. "Matthew I can't find her. I can't find Claire." Her voice sounded urgent. "What if George has done something awful to her just to keep this stupid curse going?"

Matthew stood up and rushed over to Tilly. "Don't worry, we'll find her. She can't have gone far. She's here somewhere." He glanced back at Jillian.

Jillian smiled and nodded. "Please go and help Tilly. She needs you." When they were gone Jillian turned her attention to Seth. He was reading something on the internet. "Did you find something?"

"Yes I did." Seth told her. He moved his laptop screen a bit so she could see it. There on the screen was a picture of the man they knew as George Walker. The article under the photo stated that the man was wanted for murder. It told that Beau Lamprey was wanted in New Orleans for the murder of his mother Sharon Lamprey. When he fled New Orleans he went to Natchez and got into a street brawl and stabbed another man to death. Jillian looked at the date of the article and it read 1929.

"Why would they still be looking for him today?" she asked.

"I found the article when I searched for Beau Lamprey. I also found his grandmother Chantez Lamprey. She was some kind of voodoo priestess. The article I found about her said she was into dark magic. When she died in 1975 there was quite a celebration to mourn her death."

"She must have been the one to teach George the black magic he used to curse this place." Jillian commented.

Seth began hitting the keys on his laptop and when he was finished he brought up a different site. This one contained information on time loops. There he found all sorts of information how to make one but nothing on how to stop one.

After a few minutes he growled and pushed the laptop away from him. "This is useless." Seth said.

"We can't give up." Jillian said. "There has to be something we can use."

"If there is I can't find it." Seth told her.

"Maybe it's time for a break." Jillian told him. "Maybe we should get something to eat."

Seth ran his fingers through his hair and agreed. "Okay, I'll take a break. It won't get us anywhere but maybe I do need to get away from this for a few minutes."

Jillian got up and made some coffee. Seth opened the refrigerator, looking for something to eat. He brought out some lunchmeat and cheese. For a few minutes the kitchen was quiet while they prepared a sandwich. When they sat down at the table to eat Jillian asked, "Did the article about George mention the name of the man he murdered in Natchez?"

Seth shook his head. "I don't think so. Why? What difference does the name mean?"

"I don't know if it makes any difference at all, but we have to find out all we can about George. Something tells me he's the key to unlocking the curse."

Chapter Thirteen

When he finished his sandwich Seth got the article about the man George murdered back on his computer. He read the whole article but there was no mention of who the man was he was supposed to have murdered. Jillian was disappointed. "We have to find out more about that stabbing."

"Why are you stuck on the stabbing?" Seth asked.

"Because I don't think George would have committed murder on just anyone. He would need a reason to stick a knife into someone."

"And how did you come to this conclusion?" Seth asked.

Jillian shrugged. "I don't know, it just seems right somehow. I mean I don't know the man from Adam but I just know somehow."

Seth sat down at the keyboard. He researched the papers the next day but didn't find any mention of the stabbing. He searched the internet for any other mention of Beau Lamprey but didn't find anything else. He googled Lamprey and found a reference to a Troy Lamprey. Clicking on the link it took him to another newspaper article four days after the first article. Beau was accused of murdering his brother.

Seth glanced over at Jillian. "The man Beau was

accused of murdering was his older brother Troy. It took the police four days to uncover the man's name." He read a little more of the article and said, "One witness called it self deference but there was a second man that came with Troy and he clearly called it murder, as Troy came unarmed."

"Troy was unarmed?" Jillian asked. "That doesn't make any sense. Why would George kill his own brother?"

"Are you still thinking George had a reason to kill his brother?" Seth asked.

Jillian nodded her head absently as she was trying to think of a reason why George would kill his brother. "We need to find that letter." Jillian snapped her fingers.

"What are you talking about? What letter?" Seth frowned.

"The letter of Beau's that Claire read." Jillian told him. "There must be something more in that letter."

"Woman, that letter was written over eighty years ago. It was probably destroyed in the fire. I doubt you'll find it now." Seth said.

"I know but we have to try. We need to find it if we can." Jillian insisted.

Tilly and Matthew came around the corner and into the kitchen. Jillian looked up and asked, "Did you find Claire?"

"No," Tilly said wringing her hands together. "And I'm worried about her. She's never just taken off like this before."

"She has to be here somewhere. She can't get out of the Inn." Jillian reminded her.

"Then why won't she answer my call?" Tilly asked.

Jillian shrugged. "Tilly, do you remember which room George used when he was here?"

Tilly thought for a moment. "Yes, he used the room at the end of the first floor hall, why do you ask?"

"I think the key to breaking the curse might be in the letter he got from his grandmother." Jillian told him. "I want to see if the letter still exists."

"That's a long shot." Matthew told her. "The fire may have destroyed it eighty years ago."

"I'm hoping if the Inn came back everything in the Inn came back as well." Jillian said.

"What do you need the letter for?" Tilly asked.

"Beau murdered a man shortly after receiving that letter. I don't think Beau had a choice. I think someone in his family cursed him and that curse spilled over to follow him here. I need the letter to confirm my suspicions."

"And what if you're right? What do we do then?" Tilly asked.

"We have to find a way to break the curse." Jillian said. "Let's go and see if we can find the letter." As they walked down the hall to George's old room, Jillian got the feeling she was on the right track.

Seth opened the door, as they entered they felt a coolness to the room. Jillian looked around and noticed nothing seemed out of place. She hadn't been in this room before now. So much had happened since she got here she hadn't gotten around to finishing her inspection of the Inn.

Jillian rubbed her hands over her arms. She glanced

at Seth but shook her head. She began to open the dresser drawers, pawing through George's clothing. She found he didn't have that much, two pair of jeans and a couple t-shirts. Socks and underwear were in the drawer on the left side. Glancing around the room she saw Seth going through George's possessions in the closet.

Jillian turned back to the dresser. On the top was a valet, a small built in drawer. She opened the drawer and found the letter. Pulling it out of the drawer she called out, "I think I found it."

Seth and Matthew came over to where she stood and peered over her shoulder. Jillian unfolded the letter, smoothing it out so she could read the address. It was addressed to Beau Lamprey. The mailing address was Natchez, Louisiana.

"This must be it." Jillian said as she opened the letter. As she removed the letter from the envelope something heavy came out with it. Jillian had to grab it quickly before it fell to the floor. Holding it up in the light Jillian found it was an amulet of sorts. She glanced over at Seth, before she unfolded the letter.

The words were written in a language Jillian couldn't read. She looked up at everyone and turned the letter to them. "I can't read this."

Tilly reached out her hand and tried to take the letter from her. Her hand went through the paper. She glanced up at Jillian and said, "I think I know what the letter says but I need to see it and I can't touch it."

"Let's take it back to the kitchen." Jillian said. She

lifted the amulet and stared at it. "We need to know more about this too."

A few minutes later Jillian spread the letter out for Tilly to read. She gave Seth the amulet and said, "Can you go online and see what this talisman is. There had to be a reason it was sent to George."

Jillian glanced at Tilly and asked, "Can you read it?"

Tilly glanced up at her and nodded. "The letter is written in French. As with most people from Louisiana the native language was French."

"What does it say?"

Tilly looked at the letter again. "It's from his grandmother. She's telling him there is no coming home for him. He is no longer welcome there. His father still lives but he is inches from death. She curses him telling him that the spilling of blood will continue until he is gone from this world. She tells him to watch his back; if his father dies she will send someone to extract revenge."

"That must have been what happened." Jillian concluded. "George's father died and Grandma send his brother Troy to deal with him."

"But George got Troy before Troy could kill him." Seth said. He turned the laptop toward Jillian. There on the screen was the amulet they found with the letter. "The amulet is sent to someone the High Priestess curses. It reminds the person who receives it that they are cursed. This talisman is supposed to return upon the death of the receiver."

"But that doesn't make sense. When the fire killed George eighty years ago, the talisman should have returned to his grandmother." Jillian said.

"You're forgetting that George put a curse on the Inn." Tilly reminded them. "He made it possible for everything and everyone inside the Inn to keep coming back."

"So in a sense he's cheating death." Seth suggested. "And death is the only thing in life that won't be cheated. George may have started the original fire but death is the one that keeps it going."

"I thought you didn't believe in all this stuff." Jillian reminded him.

"I think I've seen enough to open my mind to the possibilities." Seth told her.

"Does the article say anything about how to break the curse of the talisman?" Jillian asked.

Seth shook his head.

"I think if you break the talisman you'll break the curse." Claire suddenly appeared in the kitchen. She refused to look at Tilly but instead focused on Jillian.

"Where have you been? We've been looking for you." Tilly admonished her sister.

Claire finally glanced at Tilly. "I guess I just needed some alone time, time to think about everything that's happened, both recently and in the past. It was time I finally faced the truth."

"What truth are you talking about?" Tilly asked her sister.

Claire began to pace. "I had to face the fact that I wasn't as innocent as I pretended to be in all this."

"What do you mean?" Tilly asked.

Claire raised her head and looked at her sister. "I mean I wasn't as innocent as I wanted to be. I saw the way you looked at Matthew and I was jealous. I was the oldest and it was supposed to be me running away to get married, not you. I should have been the one Matthew fell in love with. I may have flirted with George just to get some attention."

"Oh Claire," Tilly whispered. "I never meant to hurt you."

Claire smiled. "I know that. In my heart I knew Matthew loved you and that you loved him. I just couldn't resist meddling." She took a deep breath. "Getting back to George, I may have led him into believing that I may have feelings for him when I knew deep down in my heart I didn't. I didn't know that much about him and he would never tell me the truth." Claire reached out to grab Tilly's hands. "All of this is my fault and if I want to clear it up I have to take responsibility for my actions."

The sisters hugged and Claire took a step back. "What are you going to do?" Tilly asked her sister.

"I'm going to try and get through to George. He's the only one of us that knows how to break the curse." Claire said. "This has to stop." She gave her sister one more hug and asked, "Wish me luck." Then she turned and disappeared.

Tilly turned her head and looked at Matthew. He

opened his arms and she went to him. When his arms went around her Tilly wept for her sister. No one knew what the outcome would be but everyone hoped for the best.

Chapter Fourteen

The night passed slowly and there was no sign of Claire or George. Whatever was happening between them was hidden from the rest of the group. Tensions were high as they waited.

They were still waiting as the sun came up over the eastern horizon. Jillian had made a pot of coffee and was pouring two cups when she turned and saw Claire standing in the doorway. One of the cups slipped from her hand and crashed to the floor.

Tilly stood and went to her. Claire looked utterly exhausted and close to tears. She melted into her sisters arms and burst into tears. Tilly glanced at Matthew and held her sister tighter.

"What happened?" Tilly finally asked.

Claire looked up at her sister. "I tried to talk to him but he said it was too late to stop what would happen in a few hours. He said the time loop would continue but this time would be the last time. This time the fire would consume the Inn and everyone in it and there was nothing we could do to stop it."

"So we only have a few hours left?" Jillian whispered.

Claire glanced over at her and nodded. "He said the magic in the amulet was strong and he couldn't beat it. The pouch he buried so long ago was a talisman that was meant to protect us, not hurt us and now that it was inside the Inn the protection wouldn't be in place. He told me we would all burn this time."

"What about the talisman he got from his grandmother? Did he say anything about that?" Seth asked.

Claire nodded. "He said at last it would return to the next High Priestess. His family would know he was dead this time. Justice would be served for them anyway."

"He's willing to just give up?" Jillian was astonished. "After all this time he's just willing to give up and accept his fate?" She began to pace. "Why now after all this time?"

"What do you mean?" Seth asked.

"There is something going on here." Jillian told them.

"What do you mean?" Matthew asked.

"George," Jillian called out. "We know you're still here. Please come out and talk to us."

Everyone waited but George didn't show up. Jillian called out again, "George, come on out. At the least we deserve to know why we're going to die."

Claire stepped out of her sister's embrace and called out, "George, please come out."

"What did you mean when you said there was something more going on here?" Seth asked.

Jillian began to pace. "I mean, if George placed the pouch in the cemetery to protect everyone, there might be another pouch hidden somewhere for the time loop. George is the only one of us that knows what the talisman means.

All we know is what the talisman is supposed to mean."

"You think there's more to the talisman than we know?" Seth asked. "Like what?"

Jillian shrugged. "I don't know but I think George does." She stopped pacing and called out, "George, what would happen if we broke the talisman your grandmother sent you?"

The black cloud appeared in the corner of the kitchen. When the cloud disappeared and George took its place he took a step toward the table. "Even if you broke the talisman you won't stop what's coming. The curse can't be stopped."

"Why? What does the talisman mean?" Jillian asked.

George shrugged. "Nothing to most people, but to someone like me, it's a death sentence."

"What do you mean someone like you?" Jillian asked.

"I grew up on the bayou in New Orleans. My family lived and breathed everything native to our culture, including voodoo. My grandmother taught us all the secrets of the ages, including the curses." He picked up the talisman. "When my father died my grandmother sent my oldest brother to hunt me down. When he died and not me I thought I was free and clear. Then the letter came and I knew I would never be free. When I came here I hid the pouch in the cemetery to hide myself from fate. I included something from each of you so the curse couldn't get to me through one of you." He paused to look at Claire. "The night of the fire do you remember what I asked you?"

"Yes, you asked me what I wanted you to do and I asked you to save me." Claire said.

George smiled. "I began to chant an old spell I learned from my grandmother. That spell began the time loop. I thought if she could use voodoo to kill me I could use it to protect the woman I came to care for."

"But?" Jillian interjected.

George turned to look at her and smiled. "The spell worked for eighty years, even after my grandmother died. The talisman means nothing. The power it had is gone. It died with my grandmother."

"So it doesn't mean anything anymore?" Jillian asked.

"Not a thing. It isn't the talisman you have to worry about." George told them.

"Then what do we have to worry about?"

George threw the talisman on the table and said, "You can't cheat death forever. When I evoked the spell Claire and I cheated death. Tilly was caught up in the spell as well but her death was natural. We all have to accept the inevitable. Death has been waiting a long time to take our souls."

"What about me?" Matthew asked. "I don't want to lose Tilly, not after all this time."

George turned to look at him. "You won't lose her. When death comes for the two of you he will take you together. Only Claire and I have to pay the price."

"Then let death come." Claire told them. "If this is

the price we have to pay then let death come. I'm ready."

George walked over to her and cupped his hand around her cheek. "If only you could have given me a chance. We could have been happy I think."

Claire looked into his eyes. "We'll never know now will we? Maybe we did cheat ourselves out of something that could have been good, but we all had our secrets. If only you had been a little more willing to share yours. Who know maybe I could have fallen in love with you, given the chance, but it's too late for that now." She pressed her hand over his and asked, "What will happen now?"

"When the fire starts Death will come for us and this time we will have no choice but to let him take us." George told her. "Maybe he will be satisfied with you and me. I don't know." George turned to look at Tilly and Matthew. "He'll take the two of you also." He turned to look at Jillian and Seth. "When the fire takes you he'll collect your souls too. This time nothing will stop him from collecting his souls. This year when the Inn burns to the ground it won't be coming back."

"What do you mean when the fire starts?" Jillian asked. "Can't you stop it? The fire doesn't have to happen this year."

George shook his head. "We died by fire eighty years ago and it's been the one constant all this time. The fire happens every year and every year for the last eighty years the fire consumes the Inn. Every year the Inn returns, every year that is except this year. This time when fire consumes the Inn it will not return. Death will come to claim our souls and the balance will be restored."

"Why can't you let us out before the fire starts?" Jillian asked.

"I told you to leave before and now it's too late." George said.

"You said that before, what did you mean?" Jillian asked.

"When I said the spell that protects the Inn, everything and everyone inside the Inn was protected by the spell. The spell seals off the Inn, nothing can get in or out until it's over." George informed them. Then he looked at Jillian and said, "I did warn you to leave before it was too late."

"So nothing will stop the fire from starting?" Jillian asked.

George shook his head. "Death has waited long enough. He won't wait any longer." He walked over to the kitchen door. Looking toward the hillside he pointed to something. Jillian and Seth went to see what he was looking at.

There on the hill was a shimmering black cloud. It was barely visible, but they could see it.

"How do we know that the cloud is death waiting?" Seth asked. "You are sometimes a black cloud."

"That's true enough but when I am in the black cloud I am death. That's how I know he's waiting out there." George told them.

"Can I ask you something?" Seth glanced at George. "If the Inn has been sealed all this time, how did you get the plantation plans out in 1962?"

"Anything is possible if you know how. I was able to briefly bend the time loop to include the town. It took a great amount of power and I found I couldn't do it again but I never had to again so it didn't matter." George told them.

"I don't understand something. If the Inn is sealed why were we able to bring Matthew's body up from the basement a few hours ago?" Jillian asked.

"Death allows only what he wants to." George told them. "As soon as you brought his body back into the Inn, Death sealed the exits."

Jillian began to pace. "So now all we can do is wait for Death to take us? There must be something we else we can do?"

"Wait a minute," Seth said. "If voodoo got us into this mess, can't you use it to get us out of it?"

George shook his head. "I don't know of a way. My grandmother might have but I don't know all her secrets." He hesitated and then said, "You don't have a choice anymore but to accept your fate."

Jillian turned her head to stare at him. There was something in the way he said, 'accept your fate' that made Jillian wonder about something. "What do you mean by that? "Accept your fate?"

George shrugged. "It is something we all have to do."

"But this isn't our fate, this is your fate." Jillian said. "This is yours and Claire, and Tilly's and Matthews's fate. Seth and I have nothing to do with this."

Claire stepped forward and laid her hand on George's arm. "Please George, help them. She's right, this is our fate not theirs."

Chapter Fifteen

George walked over to the window and looked out to the hilltop where the black shadow was waiting. Death was still there waiting. George seemed to make up his mind about something and turned back to face the others. He looked at Claire and told her, "There might be one way to get Jillian and Seth out of here, but it might also backfire and then things could be worse than they are right now." He shrugged. "Now I don't mind, I'm already dead but they might not want to take the only chance they have to live through the night."

"What are you talking about?" Jillian asked.

George turned his head and stared at her. "There is only one way I know of to get you and Seth out of the Inn before it burns but with everything else there is a price to pay for meddling with the fates."

Claire stepped closer and laid her hands on him. "Please George, please at least try to save them. Don't let them die."

George stared into her eyes and after a moment or so, he nodded. He turned back to Jillian and told her, "You have to break the talisman while I chant the spell of calling the dead."

"Who are you going to call from the dead?" Jillian asked.

"I'm going to try and make contact with my

137

grandmother. She may refuse to answer the call but it's the only way I know. My grandmother is the only person, dead or alive that could get you out of here."

Jillian glanced over at Seth and saw him nod his agreement. She turned back to George and nodded her own agreement. "Let's at least try."

George closed his eyes and tipped his head back and began to chant in the language of his ancestors. He called out his grandmother's name several times and when he opened his eyes he nodded at Jillian. Jillian threw the talisman to the floor and it shattered in several pieces. Everyone waited with bated breath for something or someone to appear.

A few minutes later a shadow began to shimmer. The shadow came and went for a moment then came and got stronger. A moment later and older woman stepped out of the shadows. She was dressed in a floor length gown of shimmering gold. Her hair was dark and it reached far down her back. Her dark eyes snapped with impatience as she looked around the kitchen. "Who dares to call me back to this world?" Her voice was husky sounding and filled with anger.

"I do, Grandmother." George spoke softly.

The woman spun around to face him. For a moment her eyes were filled with rage, then she caught herself and her head went up and she glared at him. She began to curse at him in the same language he called her with then stopped when George shook his head. "I know you are furious with me but I called you back for a reason, Grandmere."

"And what would that reason be?" she asked.

"Eighty years ago I invoked a protection spell to cheat death. I wanted the time to prove my love to a woman." George began to pace back and forth.

"So you were listening to me," Chantez smiled. "And did it work; this spell of yours?"

George looked at her and nodded. "All too well, we cheated Death for eighty years, but now the protection spell's pouch is no longer in place."

"What do you need me for? You of all people should know you can't cheat Death forever." Chantez told him.

"I know and I am willing to finally accept my own fate as are the rest of those I had protected all these years, but there are two among us that didn't die all those years ago." George turned and went to the window. He pointed outside and said, "Death waits for us but if we can't get Jillian and Seth out of the Inn they will also die. And that fate they do not deserve."

Chantez turned to look at the other people in the room with her. The bracelets on her wrist tinkled as she threw out her hand to point at them. "You would beg my help to protect outsiders rather than yourself?" She turned to look at her grandson. "Why? Why would you ask that of me?"

"I cannot ask for your forgiveness for my sin but they have not made the same sin. This is on me and me alone." George simply told her.

Chantez gazed into his eyes and read the truth there.

She shook her head and said, "We all make mistakes, Mon Amie. My mistake was believing my son was an honorable man."

"What are you saying, Grandmere?" George asked.

"The wound you inflicted on him that night didn't end his life." Chantez finally told him. "When he recovered I fully expected him to ask me to end the curse I placed on you." Chantez shook her head. Then she raised her head up proudly, "When he didn't, I lost the son I thought I raised. I sent Troy to find you to explain what happened but he never got the chance. He wasn't there to kill you; he was there to bring you home."

George's face screwed into agony. "Why didn't he tell me that? He said he was there to get revenge on my actions. He never told me our father was still alive."

Chantez nodded. "I sent your cousin with Troy and when he came back he told me what really happened that night. I tried again to get your father to remove the curse on you and again he refused. He said that any son who would try to kill his father didn't deserve redemption."

George sneered. "My father was a bastard at times."

Chantez nodded, "But a mother will always love her own, no matter what they do. I lost respect for him but he was my own flesh and blood and I loved him."

"What happened then?" George wanted to know.

"I looked for you but I could never find you." Chantez told him.

"I placed a protection spell so you wouldn't be able

to find me." George admitted.

"Your father died on September 8, 1931." Chantez told him. "He was driving to meet his whore when suddenly the truck he was in burst into flames."

George looked thunderstruck. Claire gasped. She walked over to him and laid her hand on his arm. He turned his head to look at her.

Chantez looked around at them. "Does this date mean something to you?"

George nodded. "That was the day we died in a fire."

"Mon Deau," Chantez gasped. She staggered back a step or two. "So justice was truly done." She looked at the others and said, "And now Death waits for you."

"Not for all of us." George told her.

Chantez raised her eyebrow. She turned her head to look at the two that didn't belong to the ghostly sect. She turned back to George and said, "Yes I think I can help them survive."

"What's the catch?" Seth asked.

Chantez turned her head slowly and stared at him. "What's the what?" she demanded.

"Please Grandmere, do not be angry. He doesn't know our ways." George begged. He knew all too well not to anger the woman in front of him.

Chantez turned her gaze back to her grandson. She looked over at Claire and noticed she was still hanging on his arm. "Is this the woman you sought to protect all those years ago?" she asked.

"Yes, this is she." George told her.

"Has she accepted you?"

George shook his head. "No."

"Why ever not?"

"I kept too much of my past a secret from her." George admitted. "I didn't want to frighten her and I ended up pushing her away."

"Not completely." Claire admitted. "I was beginning to care about you in life and after the fire I came to care even more. I couldn't tell you about my feeling because you were always so angry. You frightened me so much of the time I could barely talk to you."

Chantez walked over to the window and looked out the window at the hillside. She too could see the dark shadow of Death waiting to collect their souls. "He seems a little impatient."

"He has been waiting a long time." George said.

Chantez nodded as she turned back to the hillside. "We need to appease his ego."

"If you don't mind my asking, how do we appease Death?" Jillian asked. "Offer him a bribe?"

Chantez laughed out loud. "You cannot bribe Death, chere. He is not good or evil, he just is. Every one of us is born to die and Death knows this. The moment we pass over he is there waiting to take our souls. He is part of the Great Design."

"Is there any way to give him our souls so he doesn't want their souls too?" Tilly asked. "Our fate is sealed but they don't deserve to die. It's not their time."

"What did you mean when you said we had to appease his ego?" Seth asked.

"Death is the one constant in life. As soon as you are born you begin to die." Chantez shrugged. "As much as we all hate the idea, it happens to be true." She turned to her grandson. "Your protection spell hid you from Death for eighty years and Death knows this, for he too has been caught in your time loop. He has been waiting outside on that hillside for a long time. He couldn't come in and you couldn't go out." She walked over to the window and looked outside. Death was growing stronger and she could feel it. She turned to Jillian and told her, "As soon as you dug up the pouch my grandson buried Death was able to find you and he's been watching you, all of you."

"But he didn't come for me when I died." Matthew said.

Chantez shrugged. "If you died within these walls Death hasn't known it yet. This place is still under the spell until the fire comes again. Fire cleanses the sin and when the flames come this year they will cleanse away the past. Death will find your souls for the first and last time."

"That doesn't tell us how to appease Death." Jillian complained.

"To appease Death you have to respect it." Chantez told them. "You cheated Death for eighty years and this year you must stand tall and proud and welcome it with open arms. Only when Death is allowed inside will you be able to escape and not a moment before."

Jillian looked over at Seth. They both understood

what she meant. They had to wait until Death came for the others in order to escape. That also meant that death could come to them as well.

"Can you protect them until Death comes for us?" George asked.

Chantez shook her head. "I cannot. I cannot use the powers I had in life to cheat Death anymore. When Death came for me so long ago we made a deal and I cannot go back on my word. I will not lie to him anymore for I too have much to atone for." She looked over at Jillian and Seth. "If they are to survive they alone must choose their own time to escape."

'But that doesn't seem fair." Matthew sputtered.

"Death has no feelings of what's fair or not fair. I told you before he is not good or evil he just is." Chantez reminded them. "You can't bargain with Death. The only thing Death wants from you is your soul and if it is your time to go Death will take it."

Matthew looked at his nephew and Jillian and realized the helplessness of the situation. He glanced at Tilly and saw the concern in her eyes and he had to shake his head. "All these years I've waited for Death to claim me so I could see you again. I prayed for him to let me find you so we could be together again in Death as we had been in life and now it's going to cost two innocent people their lives."

"What did you just say?" Chantez asked.

Matthew turned to look at her. "I said I prayed I would find Tilly so we could be together in Death as we had been in life."

"That might be their saving grace." She told them.

"What are you saying Grandmere?" George asked.

Chantez turned to look at Claire. "Do you love my grandson?"

Claire backed away for the intensity of her stare. "I don't know."

Chantez shook her head. "You must know something after all these years. Is he someone you could love? I must know the answer now girl, we don't have any more time."

Claire looked at George and nodded. "I could love him, I think. I am very fond of him."

"You must be absolutely sure about your feelings. Death will be able to tell if you're lying or not." Chantez warned her.

"Where is all of this going?" Seth asked.

"There is only one way I know of to give you time to get out of the Inn before Death has a chance to notice you." Chantez explained. She turned to Matthew and said, "You prayed to Death to take your soul so you could be with the woman you loved in life," She turned to George, "And you used a protection spell to save the woman you loved from Death, if and only if she feels the same way for you, the four of you could blind Death for a moment or so. During that time, these two could escape."

Claire took a step back from George. There was doubt and uncertainty in her expression. "But I really don't know how I feel about him." She whispered. "I've lived with nothing in my heart but fear for so long. I just don't know how I feel."

George took a deep breath, "Maybe this will give your heart something more than fear to feel." He stepped up to her and swept her into his arms. Their lips came together and George put all his feelings for her in that one kiss.

Claire barely felt her feet lifted from the floor as wave after wave of pure passion swept over her. George had always excited her in ways she could only imagine before but now his lips singed her with desire as she melted into his embrace. His touch ignited something inside her and stroked the flames of desire even higher.

When neither of them could breathe anymore George's lips slowly left hers and he set her back down on the floor ever so carefully. His arms refused to let her go completely, yet cradled her close to his own heart.

Claire stared into his eyes and read for herself the feelings he had been hiding for so long. "Wow," she whispered. Her voice was barely audible as her throat suddenly became dry. "Can we do that again?" she asked.

George chuckled and Matthew laughed out loud. Claire turned her head to see her sister blush. "Is this what love feels like?"

Tilly's cheeks were bright pink and she nodded. "Oh that's just the beginning."

Chantez laughed at the expression on her face. "I think maybe you do love him."

Claire turned her face into George's shoulder.

"Maybe I do at that." She whispered.

Chantez clapped her hands together and told them, "Good, now this is what you need to do. When the fire starts the four of you need to form a circle by holding hands. Once the circle is formed you must not break it. You must all be of one mind to accept your fate and accept Death when he comes for you."

"I'm afraid." Tilly whispered. Her voice was low but Chantez heard her fear.

"You must not let Death see your fear." Chantez told her. "Death must concentrate on your souls and overlook the other two. You must be brave and accept your fate."

Matthew took her hand and raised it to his lips. He gently kissed her fingers. "Can you do this for us? Can you give yourself to death so we may be together?"

"I hope so." She told him. "I love you more than life itself. I waited for you to come back for me I guess I can do this too."

"When did the fire start?" Chantez asked her grandson.

George looked at the clock on the kitchen wall and said, "The fire will start anytime now."

Chantez went to the window and glanced at the hillside. The black cloud she'd seen there earlier had grown deeper in color and bigger than before. "Death is getting ready to take you."

There was a crash in the living room and everyone could smell the scent of kerosene. The smell of smoke came next as the flames began. George and Claire moved closer to Matthew and Tilly. The girls hugged one last time and the four of them clasped hands together.

"I will see you on the other side." Chantez told them. As she moved away from the circle she lifted her head and began to chant. Soon she faded away into the nothingness of the underworld.

Jillian couldn't believe this was happening. She watched as the flames began licking their way from the living room to the rest of the Inn. The smoke was getting more noticeable now and she grabbed Seth's hand and began backing away from the door. She could feel the heat from the fire in front of them. She knew they were trapped and there was no way out of the Inn. Seth pulled her down to the floor where the air was a little clearer. Brandy nuzzled her hand and crept closer to her

Jillian coughed. Sweat beaded on her forehead as the fierce heat from the flames began to make it way closer to them. Jillian felt weak. The air was so thick with smoke she couldn't breathe. She looked over to where Matthew and the others were standing. All four were still holding hands and all four had their faces turned upwards.

She glanced over at Seth and saw that he too was watching the group. Turning her head back to them she gasped out loud. All four of them were shimmering in a white glow and slowly all four of them became solid again. They were all young again even Matthew who had lived to become an old man.

"What the hell?" Seth whispered. "What's

happening to them?"

"I think Death just turned back the clock. This is what would have been eighty years ago." Jillian whispered. She didn't want the spell to be broken by her words.

The air was thicker now and the wisps of smoke rose to the ceiling and began pouring downward. They could all feel the heat from the flames.

Jillian could see Matthew tighten his grip on Tilly's hand. They could see her trembling as the fire got closer. Soon the flames were licking at their feet. One by one the flames engulfed their bodies. Each of them screamed as the pain from the fire took them. Jillian put her hands over her ears to hide from the noise but it echoed in her mind.

Chapter Sixteen

The fire was reaching out for whatever it could consume in the kitchen and Jillian saw a bright light appear behind her. Closing her eyes against the light she could almost feel the flames coming for her when she suddenly felt someone grab her arm and pull her through to the light. She prepared her body for the worst but when she opened her eyes again she was laying on the lawn outside. She sat up and looked around. Seth was beside her and Brandy was romping around in the grass.

Jillian turned her head and stared at Seth sitting in the grass staring at her. "Did we make it?"

"I think so." He told her.

Jillian glanced over at the house. She could see the damage the fire had done. Wisps of smoke still smoldered but the Inn was gone. The fire this time, just like the first time, had been real.

"Did you feel something just before the door opened?" he asked her.

Jillian turned to stare at him briefly before she looked away. "Yes I felt it. It was Death coming to claim my soul."

"That's what I thought too." Seth admitted. "Then I felt something grab my hand and I was out here."

Jillian's head snapped back to stare at him. "Something grabbed your hand? Didn't you grab my arm and pull me out of there?"

Seth shook his head. "When I opened my eyes the Inn was gone, burned to the ground. When I felt someone grab my hands the place was burning but it wasn't gone. We went somewhere for a little while anyway."

Jillian got to her feet and stared at what was left of the Inn. There was nothing left of the building but ashes. Time had stood still for her and Seth at least for a little while. She didn't understand what had happened.

She turned to look at Seth and saw him shrug. "I don't know any more about what happened to us than you do. When I woke up we were both out here."

Then they both turned to the rubble of the building and saw a white shimmer growing from the debris. The shimmer grew until it became a bright light. Someone stepped out of the light and manifested into human form. She was a young woman and as she stepped closer to them she smiled. "My name is Destiny and I have come with a message for you."

Jillian looked at Seth and then looked back at Destiny. "Yes I was the one that pulled you from the flames of Death. It wasn't your time to die."

"Are you fate?" Jillian asked.

Destiny shook her head. "No I am not fate, I am an angel sent to you from someone you love to give you a message."

"What's the message?" Jillian asked.

"George and Claire, Matthew and Tilly wanted you to know they reached the other side. They all send their love for what you helped them accomplish. You helped to right a wrong against the natural order of things and they are grateful."

"What about Death? Is he grateful that we cheated him?" Seth asked.

Destiny smiled. "But you didn't cheat Death. It wasn't your time to die yet and Death knew this. He wasn't here to claim your souls."

"Then why couldn't we get out of the Inn?" Jillian asked.

"Fate sealed the doors to the Inn a long time ago. When George enchanted the Inn in a time loop Fate had no choice but to do everything it did the night of the first fire." She turned and looked at the smoke and ashes. "Now everything is and will remain the way it was supposed to be."

Jillian had to ask, "And the others? Are they where they are supposed to be as well?"

Destiny turned back to her and said, "Yes they are. George has some explaining to do to the powers that be but they are all together. And yes Claire was really meant for George. She is his soul mate. Fear held her for so long she couldn't determine her own feelings but now she's very happy with him."

"What about George's father?" Seth asked.

"George's father is another story all together. He lied to his family about the real reason he was beating his wife that night and now he has to pay for his lies and deception."

"What was the real reason?" Jillian asked.

"Dark magic took his soul and instead of fighting it he gave into his temptations. He was seeing another woman and breaking his vows to his wife. The other woman was truly evil and when he died she died as well. Both of their souls went to hell."

Jillian looked at Seth then looked back at Destiny. "What about Chantez? Didn't she practice black magic in her voodoo as well?"

Destiny shook her head. "Chantez was using the good magic of voodoo to defend against the dark magic. She knew the truth about her son from the moment he met the witch that destroyed him. She could see the aura of death on his soul but because she loved him, she couldn't say anything about it. When he died she made sure the witch that enslaved him suffered the same fate he did."

"This is all so confusing." Seth commented as he shook his head.

"This is not something that mortals, such as you were supposed to know about." Destiny told them. "The powers that be are giving you a glimpse into their world only because of what you did here tonight."

"What happens to us next?" Jillian asked.

Destiny hesitated for a moment then said, "The powers that be would ask one more thing from you. You don't have to agree to their request."

Jillian glanced at Seth then looked back at Destiny. "What do they want from us?"

"A long time ago a gem was of great importance

taken from them. A mistress of Darkness spirited the gem away from their safe keeping. They believe this woman is the same woman that tempted George's father, Leon. When the witch died, they thought the gem had been lost for all time."

"But it wasn't was it?" Jillian surmised.

"No it wasn't." Destiny told them. "When George went to answer for his actions he saw the stones of reality and noticed one of them was missing. He told the powers that be about a locket he'd seen a woman wearing. He didn't know the woman was a witch enslaving his father. He noticed the locket because of the unusual coloring of the stone."

"How big is the stone?" Jillian asked.

"They are small, only about the size of a dime, but the stones have hidden powers and they are supposed to be used for good. The witch was using hers to change what must be. She sought to join with the Lamprey's magic to increase her own powers. She thought if she were strong enough she could challenge the powers that be."

"But if she died when Leon did, what happened to the locket?" Jillian asked.

"That's what you must find out. George said after he left the glade he looked back and saw the witch suddenly appear. When she saw his mother she began to laugh. She was wearing the locket."

"Why can't they just call the stone back to them?" Seth asked.

Destiny looked over at him. "The powers that be

cannot interfere with mortal affairs. Since a mortal took the stone a mortal must return it. They can only request that you go after the stone."

"And if we do go after the stone, what happens then?" Jillian asked.

"The balance shall be restored." Destiny told her. She seemed to be waiting for another question but it never came. She reached into the pocket of her robe and brought out a jewel. Handing it to Jillian she told them, "This jewel will be your guide. When you get close to the stone this jewel will begin to glow."

Jillian wanted to reach out for the jewel but she hesitated briefly and looked over at Seth. "Are you up for another adventure or has this one been enough for you?"

Seth looked at both women. He began this trip a total non-believer but so much has happened since he arrived, he wasn't sure what he believed anymore. "Would you tell my uncle something for me? Would you tell him that I think I finally believe? He showed me a world I never knew existed and that true love really does last through eternity. I'm glad he found his Tilly and I hope he's finally at peace."

Destiny smiled. "I'll tell him."

Jillian reached out and Destiny gave her the stone. She looked over at Seth and said, "I guess we're going to New Orleans."

"What happens if we manage to find the stone?" Seth asked.

"I will find you again and retrieve it." Destiny told

them. "I have one more thing for you. Chantez wants to help. She would like to give you something." Destiny turned a little to her left and waved her hand. The air began to shimmer and Chantez appeared beside Destiny. She looked at Jillian and reached for her hand.

"So you are going after the stone?" She asked Jillian.

Jillian nodded. "We're going to try."

Chantez took a ring off her hand and held it out to Jillian. "I want to tell you a story about my family. We believe in voodoo and our family has always practiced the religious aspects of the craft. Our voodoo is good voodoo, not the bad one. We believe the witch Leon was seeing used black voodoo to enslave him. The night he beat his wife, he was under her spell. When Beau stood up to him, Leon couldn't stand it. If Beau hadn't stabbed him, I think Leon would have killed him. We were under the impression Leon's wife was cheating on him so my husband killed Leon's wife and we carried Leon home. I was fearful for my son's life so the next few days were nothing but a blur. When my son began to recover from his wound I noticed several small things that didn't make much sense before. That's when I found evidence of the witch. We also found out Leon had lied to us about his wife."

"Why do you call her a witch?" Jillian asked.

"Because that is what she is." Chantez claimed. "In voodoo there are several levels of rankings. "I am a High Priestess, Santé Willows was a witch. She sought to gain the High Priestess level by enslaving my son. If Leon married her she would have used her power to gain in status. She would have combined her power with ours and used her power against us. As it was when Beau died in the fire he cursed his father. When Leon began to burn I invoked the spell that took his lover's life."

"What happened after that?" Seth wanted to know.

"After Sante's death her power would have transferred to the next in her line, just as my power transferred to my daughter Channel. But this ring I couldn't give to her. We are still under Sante's family's curse. But now with your help, that curse can be lifted and things can be set right."

"What things need to be set right?" Jillian asked.

"I think the Willow's source of power is from the Stone. It protects their family and has for some time. Without the stone they can finally be held accountable for everything they've done."

Jillian quickly glanced at Destiny then said, "Are you looking for vengeance or justice?"

Chantez laughed out loud. "No cherie, it's not vengeance I seek. I want the witch to pay the full price for her deviltry. She turned to black voodoo to gain stature and that is wrong. I need to cleanse the stain from my family and to do that I have to take away her power." She handed her ring to Jillian. "You go to my family and they will help you find the witch. When you have gotten her power, the stone, you give this ring to my granddaughter Sarene. My daughter passed her power to Sarene a few years ago. She will know what to do with it."

Jillian hesitated to take the ring from her. She really didn't want to get caught up in a family feud between two families, both of whom were comfortable using voodoo. She didn't understand the complexities of the religious aspects versus the black magic aspects.

Chantez noticed her hesitation and cocked her head to one side. "Why do you hesitate? I am offering you the deal of a lifetime."

"Maybe that's why I hesitate." Jillian told her. "The ring is something you should have given to your family, not me."

Chantez nodded. "I understand, but I told you why I didn't. This ring has the power that you will need to identify the witch that placed a curse on my family. Only you can help destroy that curse. My family needs your help."

Jillians looked into her eyes and saw no vengeance in them, only hope for the future. She reached out and took the ring. Placing it on her finger she felt a surge of power flowing through her. She quickly glanced at Chantez, only to see her smile.

"Ah, you feel the power of the ring don't you?" She nodded. "The ring is powerful and in the right hands will do good things, but in the wrong hands the ring will increase the wearer's power beyond belief. I could not take the chance to pass the ring down. Santé was getting too close." Chantez paused and then added, "The fact that you don't believe in voodoo will help you when it counts. Don't be fooled though. In the final showdown what you do truly believe will either help or hinder you?"

Jillian stared at her. "What the heck does that mean?"

"You will know when the time is right, not until then." Chantez warned them.

Jillian glanced over at Seth. "Are you still willing to go to New Orleans with me?"

At Seth's nod, Jillian glanced back at Chantez and asked, "How do we find your family?"

"My family owns a home right off Bourbon Street. Just go there and explain your quest and they will help you."

When Jillian nodded her agreement Destiny and Chantez began to shimmer again and a few moments later they disappeared.

"Wow," Seth ran his finger through his hair. "Three days ago I would have laughed if someone told me ghosts and spirits were real."

"I know; all of this is somehow so unreal." Jillian glanced down at her finger and the ring she now wore. "Hopefully we are doing the right thing."

"You still have doubts, don't you?" Seth asked.

Jillian turned to him. "Don't you?"

"Maybe, but we did agree to try." Seth reminded her.

"I know." Jillian took a deep breath. "I'm sorry Matthew is gone."

Seth glanced at her. "Don't be, he's finally happy. From the time I can remember Matthew has been searching for something. I never understood that until now. I guess I've never known a love as strong as that."

"I know what you mean." Jillian told him. "My grandmother asked me to find out the truth about what happened the night of the fire. I guess we found out more than we both bargained for."

Seth glanced down at her hand. "So are we really going on another adventure or what?"

Jillian looked down at the jewel. "I guess we are."

Part II
Chapter Sixteen

New Orleans was hot and the breezes off the gulf made it unbearably humid Jillian found as they walked down Bourbon Street. The historical ambiance of New Orleans flooded her soul as she walked the French Quarter. She could feel the echoes of the past with each step she took.

They checked into a motel a few hours ago and now they were seeing New Orleans. Most of the city was still being repaired after the Hurricane but repairs were slow. Jillian looked at the buildings around her. The brick and mortar was held together by hundreds of years of history.

As they walked down the street the ring on Jillian's finger began to throb. As the throbbing got stronger Jillian allowed it to lead them past the shops and taverns. When they reached the corner of Bourbon and St. Louis Streets they turned and walked half a block. The ring stopped throbbing and Jillian glanced at Seth, and then turned to look at the house in front of them. It was a three story building with a balcony on the top two floors and a full front porch. The house itself looked as old as the city.

As they stood there looking at the house the front door opened and an older man walked out. He stared at them for a moment and walked closer.

Jillian and Seth waited for him and the closer he got

the more nervous Jillian got. "Can I help you?" he asked.

"Are you any relation to Chantez Lamprey?" Jillian asked.

The man frowned. "Chantez was my mother. I am Benjamin Lamprey." He paused then added, "How did you hear about my mother?"

Jillian quickly glanced at Benjamin. "We met her a few days ago."

"That's impossible. My mother died a long time before you were even born." Benjamin's voice was harsh as his stare turned into a scowl.

"I know," Jillian told him. "But it's true. We met her spirit and she asked us to come here."

"I don't believe you." Benjamin said. "I think it's time you leave."

"Before you toss us out, maybe you should see this." Jillian told him as she held out her hand. When Benjamin's eye found his mother's ring he gasped.

Grabbing her hand he pulled it closer as he stared at the ring. He looked up at her pale face and growled, "Where did you get this?"

"I told you your mother gave it to me." Jillian told him. She pulled her hand out of his grasp and rubbed her crushed fingers.

"Maybe you should come inside while we discuss this." Benjamin suggested as he bowed toward the house.

As Jillian walked to the front porch she knew she was being watched. She didn't know how many pairs of eyes were glued to her but she could feel a slight hostility beyond the forbidding looking doors. Benjamin stepped around her to open the huge wooden doors of the house and motioned her inside.

The house was surprising cool. The foyer was tiled with Spanish tiles. Their muted colors lent a calming effect as you walked into the great room. The furniture in the great room would have looked bulky in any other room but here it looked like it belonged.

As they walked into the great room Jillian found herself facing several other people. Benjamin took a step or two to separate himself from Jillian and Seth. He stood with the other members of his family. He turned his head toward the others and announced, "This is my family. My older brother Jean," Benjamin nodded toward an older man sitting on the sofa. "And his wife Millicent. My sister Channel, her daughter Sarene, her son Eric, and lastly my wife Lisa Marie."

Everyone stared at them and Jillian felt uncomfortable. Taking a deep breath she told them, "My name is Jillian Levy and this is Seth Nixen. We have come here to ask you for help. Two days ago we met a man named Beau Lamprey."

Benjamin and Jean gasped out loud. They looked at each other and then back at Jillian. "How could you have met Beau? He died a long time ago."

"Yes he did. Eighty years ago to be exact." Jillian told them.

"Yet you say you met him?" Channel asked.

"Yes, we did." Jillian said.

"Jean and I weren't ever born yet when Beau disappeared." Benjamin admitted.

"And I was a child of two. Leon was so much older than we were." Channel admitted.

"I know." Jillian admitted. "He was caught in a time loop of his own making when we met."

"A time loop? I don't understand." Jean questioned. "What does a time loop have to do with anything?"

"Please be patient. I'll explain but I have to do it in my own way." Jillian told them.

"Please continue." Sarene said.

"After Beau killed his brother Troy in Natchez, he went north. He changed his name and began a new life. He thought he was banned from coming back here so he began a new life. When someone he cared for was facing death he invoked a time loop to save her and himself."

"Then my uncle came back to face his own past and the time loop was broken." Seth intervened. "To stop death from taking our souls he called on your mother for help. She helped us and him and then asked us to help her and you." Jillian could see the doubt on their faces. She held out her hand and showed them the ring. "She gave me this ring so you would be open to the possibility that I'm not here to take anything away from you."

Channel got up and walked over to her. She looked at the ring for a moment then asked, "What did she want you to do?"

"She wanted me to ask you to help me stop the witch that enslaved your brother Leon." Jillian dropped her bomb.

Channel gasped and took a step backward. Benjamin stepped up to catch his sister and led her back to the couch. Sarene checked on her mother then stood up. "What makes you think we can help you? This witch is very powerful."

"I know. Chantez told me, but she also told me that if we can get the stone she wears in a locket around her neck, she won't be so powerful. Chantez thinks the stone in the locket is the base of her power."

"Why would my grandmother give you the ring that is the base of our family's power?" Sarene asked.

"She gave me the ring so I could get the stone back with your help. She thinks if we can get the stone back we can remove the curse from your family." Jillian told them. "How else would I have gotten the ring?"

"Indeed, how else would you have gotten the ring?" Jean asked.

"I've heard the stories about Uncle Leon and his witch," Eric said. "When she died the same day Leon died her power was transferred to her sister Cassandra. A few years ago Cassandra transferred the powers and the locket to her daughter Megan."

"Then its Megan we have to find. She will have the locket." Seth said.

"That might not be as easy as you might think." Eric told them.

"What do you know that we don't?" Jean asked his nephew.

"I've been following Megan for a while now and I've seen her communicate with the spirit of Santé." Eric said.

"How do you know it's Sante`s spirit?" Channel asked.

"I could feel the evil emanating from her." He said. "I overheard their conversation too. Santé was telling Megan how to complete a spell to take over another clan's power."

"When was this?" Benjamin demanded.

"About three days ago." Eric admitted. He turned to look at Jillian and Seth. "Santé was telling Megan she needed the blood of someone who had worn the ring. Megan told her aunt that no one in our clan other than Chantez had ever worn the ring and Santé laughed. She told Megan that someone would come to us wearing the ring lost so long ago."

"She knew Jillian was coming? How would she know that?" Channel asked.

"There is much about the spirit world we don't know." Jean admitted. "If it's possible for Mother to get through to someone on this side why would Santé not be able to? Santé used black magic in her lifetime, surely the black magic would provide a way to make and maintain a connection."

"Did my mother ever tell you why she didn't pass the ring of power onto anyone in her family?" Channel asked.

"Yes she did but I'll explain that later. Right now we have to locate Megan." Jillian told them.

"She has gone to the bayou every evening for the last week or so." Eric offered. "That's where she meets Santé."

"Then I guess we'll get there first.' Seth told them. "Can you show us the way?" He asked Eric.

Eric glanced at the faces of his family and turned to look at Seth. "Yes I can show you the way."

"And I will go with you." Sarene told them. "I think you will need the protection I can give you."

"And you will need the protection the ring will give you." Channel told her daughter.

Sarene looked at her mother. "What do you mean?"

"I mean the ring offers protection from the dark side to its wearer and those close to her." Channel said. "My mother also said that whoever was wearing the ring would be the only one who could take it off her hand."

"Be careful out there tonight." Benjamin told Jillian. "If Santé knows you're there she won't hesitate to kill you. If she gets my mother's ring she will hold the power."

"Don't worry, she won't get the ring." Jillian vowed.

Chapter Seventeen

Eric and Sarene had taken them to a part of the bayou right next to the Gulf. It was hot and humid and the lush vegetation that hid them from the rest of the world offered no relief. It was getting close to the time when Megan would come to visit with her aunt Santé.

"So can you tell us more about what happened when you met our grandmother?" Sarene said. "We never got to know our cousin Beau or our uncle Leon."

"I was surprised to find any of Chantez's family alive, to be truthful." Jillian told them.

Sarene smiled. "My grandmother is a surprising woman. She gave my grandfather two families. She had Leon and another son, Arthur very earlier in their marriage. Leon was almost a grown man when she gave birth to our mother and Uncle Jean. Then a few years after they were born she had Uncle Benjamin."

"What happened to Arthur?" Seth asked.

"He died as a child from a fever." Eric told them.

"It sounds like your family had its ups and downs just like everyone else." Jillian said.

Sarene shook her head. "Not like everyone else. My grandmother was the High Priestess of a very old religion. People are afraid of voodoo for a reason. In the religion form it's as strong as your Christianity, but it's the black arts that people fear. Strong people can use the black arts of voodoo for their own gain and sometimes it works for a little while but eventually it will turn on them and suck them dry."

"What Santé has done to our family in the past stained her soul." Eric said. "When Uncle Leon died in a fire Grandmother made sure she suffered his fate as well. Her soul was damned and it was a fitting end for her."

"Do you know how long she's been visiting with Megan?" Jillian asked.

"Cassandra passed her power over to Megan four years ago." Eric told them. "I was in the same class as Megan so I knew her before all this started. I ran into Megan shortly after she got her powers and she told me about it." Eric shook his head. "I don't think she had any idea what she was getting into. I ran into her again a few weeks later and she was changed. She wasn't the young woman I knew. It was almost as if she was in a trance but I don't think she wanted to be. There was some part of her new life she was fearful of."

"She must have found something about her new life she didn't like." Sarene said.

"Maybe she's not lost yet." Seth told them. "If she's doing this against her will, it may not be too late for her to change."

"I think her aunt is pulling her strings." Eric said. "When she comes here she falls into a trance and Santé talks through her."

Sarene looked at her brother. "You seem to know a lot about her."

Eric stared at his sister for a moment. "She was at one time a very good friend of mine. I can't just let her go."

"Can you explain her ritual when she comes here? Step by step, I mean?" Jillian asked. "Maybe there is something we can use against them when the time comes."

"You can see for yourself." Eric motioned toward the clearing. "She's here."

They all turned and watched as a young woman came into the clearing. She knelt to the four corners of the globe, finally settling to the west. There was a circle of stones in front of her with chunks of wood waiting to be burned. The sun was slipping beneath the western skies when she raised her hands and began to chant.

She took a small bottle from her belt and opened it. She raised it high in the skies and then drank from it. She tipped her head back and continued the chant. Moments later the wood in the pit burst into flames and another figure appeared in the bright orange flames.

Sarene gasped. "Oh my god, that's Santé." She whispered.

As the flames in the fire grew higher Santé reached out her hand and touched the locket around her neck to the one around Megan's neck. Then she stepped out of the flames to stand next to her niece. Santé stroked the younger woman's hair as she circled her body.

They all watched as the girl fell deeper into the hypnotic trance. When Santé stepped back she gazed at the girl and began to laugh out loud.

"Damn," Sarene swore softly. "We have to get out

of here before she finds us. We can come back tomorrow."

Jillian turned her head and stared at Sarene. "What does it all mean?" she whispered.

"Grab my hand and don't let go until we're clear of here." Sarene told them. "Don't let go or she'll find you."

Jillian, Eric and Seth grabbed her hand and let her lead them away from the bayou. A few blocks away they stopped and Sarene faced them all. "Ok sister spill it. What happened back there?"

Sarene began to pace as she thought about what she'd just witnessed. "Santé is a very smart witch. She was prepared for anything back in her day."

"What does that mean?" Jillian asked.

"She carries a part of the stone you came here to get and Megan carries the other part. Only when the two halves are joined can she step out of her world into ours."

"What happened to Megan back there?" Eric asked. "It looked as if she had no control of what she was doing."

"She didn't." Sarene told him. "Santé has complete control over her. When she came here she was under a spell. The potion she drinks deepens the spell to the point that Santé controls everything she does. Then Santé steps out of the spirit world into ours."

Sarene looked at her brother, "Megan is in real trouble here. We have to help her but first we have to find out if she's a pawn or a willing participant."

"Do you think she could actually be part of this, if she knew what she was doing?" Eric argued. "She wouldn't do this willingly."

"I don't know the girl that well." Sarene told him. "Do you? Do you know for sure she's an unwilling pawn?"

"You guys can argue this later; right now we have work to do." Jillian told them. "We need to get both lockets. The stone must be whole when we give it back to Destiny."

"That's going to be near impossible." Sarene shook her head.

"Why?" Seth asked.

"Megan must bring her aunt from her world into ours and the stone must be taken before it's joined." Sarene warned them. "That means we have to be there when she calls her aunt and I don't see that happening."

Eric pulled them into the shadows when he saw something. Sarene turned to see what his brother was looking at. It was Megan coming out of the bayou. She walked like she was still in the trance. Eric glanced at his sister. "I'm going to follow her and find out what she's up too." He took off after Megan.

Sarene shook her head. "Come on we need to let the family know what we found out. Maybe they have some suggestions." Sarene got up and walked the few blocks to the family home.

A few minutes later they found themselves in the middle of a family discussion. Jillian and Seth were silent as Sarene explained what they found.

"Santé is using her niece as a conduit from her world into ours." Sarene said. "Eric thinks Megan is an unwilling pawn and I have to say, I think he could be right."

"Why do you think so?" Benjamin asked.

Sarene began to pace as she explained. "She arrives in the bayou almost in a trance, and then she drinks a potion that puts her deep into a trance. She calls to her aunt and when Santé appears she touches two lockets together and then she steps out of the flame into our world."

"Where is Eric?" Jean asked his niece.

"He followed Megan when she came out of the bayou to see where she was going." Sarene said.

"If he gets too close to her he could get caught up in her spell." Channel warned.

"Try telling him that, Mother. I think he's got feeling for her." Sarene told her mother.

Channel looked at her brothers with fear in her eyes. History seemed to be repeating itself. "We can't let Eric make the same mistakes Leon did."

"I agree." Jean stated.

"How can we use what we've learned to get both stones back?" Jillian asked.

They all turned to her. "First we have to find out if Santé felt your presents tonight." Channel suggested.

"Why is that important?" Seth asked.

"If she did notice you were there she'll be extra careful." Jean told her. "She'll be able to sense Mother's ring and the powers that go with it. She's always coveted the ring and the powers for her own and she tried to get Leon to get them for her." He hesitated then went on to say,

"You may not know this part of our family history but Santé got close to the ring again. Using her powers from the spirit world she trapped our father in a limbo, somewhere between her world and ours."

"How did she do that?" Jillian asked.

"None of us know how she did it. Mother was furious when Dad disappeared. She spent the next five years of her life tracking Santé to hell and back."

"Did she ever get her husband back?" Seth asked.

Jean shook his head. "Mother died before she could get him back. That was one of the reasons she didn't pass the ring down. Every day for five years she tried everything she knew to get our father back to her but in the end she couldn't find a way to bring him back. She died knowing he's still out there somewhere."

"Oh dear lord…" Jillian exclaimed. She glanced at Seth. "She never said a word about her husband being part of the situation."

"She wouldn't have mentioned it." Benjamin said. "Mother would have put her own troubles behind any threat. She would have known that getting the locket and destroying Santé would come first. That's the sort of woman she was."

"Even if destroying Santé meant her husband was lost forever, that's what she would have done." Channel added.

"Maybe that's why she didn't mention him before." Seth surmised.

Eric joined them with a slam of the front door. He

came rushing into the room and stopped short when he saw them all there.

"Well, what did you find out?" Sarene asked.

He ran his fingers through his hair and shook his head. "I don't think she knows what she doing." He announced. "I waited until she was far enough away from the bayou to speak to her and when I touched her arm I got a shock. She looked at me as if she didn't know me for a moment then she blinked and came out of it. She didn't know where she was, I could see it in her eyes."

"What does that mean?" Jillian asked.

"It could mean Megan has no idea what her aunt is doing through her." Channel said.

"And that means we could have an innocent to save as well as a stone to get our hands on." Sarene announced.

"This is getting more and more complicated." Seth growled.

Chapter Eighteen

"When you saw Megan tonight did she seem okay to you?" Jillian asked Eric.

"What do you mean?" He asked.

"Did she seem normal to you?" she repeated her question.

"I guess so." Eric admitted. "Why do you ask?"

"We have to find a way to explain to her what we saw tonight. Your uncles agree with you, they don't think she knows she's being used. If she is innocent she needs to know the truth about what her aunt is doing to her." Jillian explained.

"I was hoping you would want to help." Eric announced. "She's waiting for us outside." Eric left the room for a moment and returned with Megan.

"You can't bring her here." Channel cried. "Not like this."

Megan looked at the people assembled in the room and turned to Eric. "Maybe this isn't a good idea."

Eric looked at her and said, "Yes it is. If anyone can help you they can."

Megan looked at him then turned back to them. "I don't know what you think of me but I swear I had no idea what I was doing out on the bayou tonight. I don't even remember how I got out there."

"What is the last thing you remember?" Jean asked.

"I came home from work as usual and my mom asked how my day went. While I was telling her about my day she made us a cup of tea. Then she suggested I lay down for a while. I went to my room and I fell asleep and the next thing I know Eric is standing next to me on the street and its dark outside."

Channel looked at her brothers and then at Megan. "What kind of tea did your mother give you?"

Megan shrugged. "She mixes different herbs together and brews it into tea, some days it's sweet and some days its lavender, rosemary. I never know until I drink it."

"What difference does that make?" Jillian asked.

Channel glanced at her. "There are herbs that when combined can act as a sleeping agent, even an agent that would lend to suggestive reasoning. If her mother gave her these herbs to get her into a suggestive state of mind she could be calling Santé from the spirit world unknowingly."

Megan began shaking her head. "Why would my mother do this to me?"

"Maybe she's not aware she's doing it either." Benjamin suggested. "Santé was a powerful witch. She could have had this all set up before she died."

"How? She didn't know she would die so young." Megan told them.

"Oh I had a feeling she knew something would happen." Channel scoffed. "Santé was not a stupid woman; she knew there would be repercussions from her attempt to sway Leon away from his family."

"My mother feared Santé." Megan said. "When Santé got her powers and turned to the black magic, mother went to the old ones for am amulet to protect her from Santé's powers. She thought she was protected until the day Santé died. When she received Santé's locket my mother changed. I watched her change from a loving, caring woman to one who only cared about one thing, black magic."

"Santé found a way to stay in control even after her death." Channel said.

"She split the stone and uses it to control her sister and her niece." Jillian reasoned.

"Why would she do something like that?" Megan wanted to know.

"She's after this," Jillian said as she held out her hand to show Megan the ring Chantez had given her.

Megan glanced at the ring on Jillian's finger and then she looked at Jillian. "This is the first time the ring has been on anyone's finger but the High Priestess of the clan. Why did Chantez give it to you?"

"Never mind that now, can you call your aunt anytime you want or only at a certain part of the day?" Jillian asked.

"Why would I want to call my aunt?" Megan shuddered. "She terrified me in life and now you're telling me she's controlling me in death."

"Tell me something, where did you get your locket?" Sarene asked Megan. "It's a very unusual colored stone."

Megan glanced down at the stone in her locket. "This locket has been in our family for years. It's gotten passed down to mother and daughter for over a hundred years. I think Santé' got it first from her mother, then when she died it came to my mother and eventually she gave it to me."

"Your aunt uses the stone inside to step from the spirit world back into our world." Jillian told her. "She broke the stone and she has one piece and you have the other piece. Only when you call to her spirit and she connects the two halves can she come back to our world."

Megan reached for the chain around her neck to take off the locket. Then she paused and asked, "I can't just give you the locket can I?"

Channel shook her head. "That locket is to you what my mother's ring is to us. Right now it's only a locket but we need both parts of the stone, not just one."

Megan thought for a moment, then said, "I need to call my aunt one more time don't I?"

"Yes you do." Sarene told her. "Can you do it?"

"I don't have a choice." Megan said. "I won't like it but I'll do it." She looked at Eric and asked, "Promise me one thing though will you?"

"What's that?"

"Promise me you'll stop her. She's evil and always has been. My mother was afraid of Sante's power, even when she received it after Sante's death."

"We will do our best to stop her." Eric promised.

"You have to do more than that." Megan warned

them. "If Santé finds out I betrayed her she'll send me to a hell I don't want to go to. Then she'll destroy your entire family."

Channel got to her feet and left the room. She returned a few minutes later with a small vial. "I want you to drink this before you call Santé. This will stop her from putting you into a trance and you will be in complete control."

"What is it?" Megan asked.

"It's an herbal tonic to neutralize the potion you drink when you get to the bayou." Channel told her.

Megan's hand went to a secret pocket in her belt and pulled out a small bottle. She seemed amazed to find it in her hand. "My god, I didn't know it was there."

Channel nodded. "She has more control over you than you realize."

"Let's get this over with," Megan said. "Before I lose my nerve." She turned and walked from the room.

"Let's hope this works, for all our sakes." Eric told them. "Come on we have to be ready for Santé."

Everyone followed him to the bayou. They found Megan already there. She stood in front of the fire pit waiting for them to get settled. They would be hidden from view yet ready to lend their support.

Megan stood alone on the bayou. She tipped her head back and began to chant a language older than time. She lifted a small vial to her lips and tipped it back. Dropping the vial to the ground she took a second vial from her pocket and raised it to her lips, before she threw the vial on the logs in the pit. She knelt to the four corners on the bayou and when she was back where she started she raised her hand and finished the chant.

Flames burst from the pit and a moment later Sante's spirit reached through the flames to touch her locket with Megan's. When she stepped through the flames and onto the sand Santé circled her niece. "Why have you come again so soon, my child?"

"I have come to ask you a question." Megan told her.

"What do you seek to know?" Santé asked as she circled the girl.

"I wanted to ask how long you have been in control of me?"

Santé stopped in her tracks, turned and came to stand in front of her. "What did you ask?" she demanded.

"How long have you controlled my movements?" Megan wouldn't back down from her stand against her aunt.

Santé looked into her niece's eyes and finally noticed they weren't glazed over like they normally would be. "What trickery is this?"

"No trickery on my part." Megan told her aunt. "You are the one who used trickery to gain what you should have lost a long time ago. You can't straddle two worlds forever."

"My, my, now who have you been talking to, I wonder." Santé commented. She placed her hand on Megan's shoulder and closed her eyes. Tipping her head back she began to hum. A few minutes later Santé broke contact with Megan and backed away in horror. "You have betrayed me."

Megan turned her head to stare at Santé. "What are you talking about?"

"You have been with the Lamprey's haven't you?" Santé snarled.

"I know Eric Lamprey from school, why do you ask?"

***

Channel looked at her brothers. "We have to stop this. Santé will kill her niece if she thinks the girl betrayed her."

Jillian held out her hand. "We have to give the girl a chance to prove herself."

"Please give her a chance." Eric pleaded. "I know she can do this."

"Get ready, just in case this goes wrong." Jean told them.

Channel looked at them and said, "Let's hope she can pull this off. We have no idea how strong Santé has become and we'll only have one chance to get this right."

***

Santé curled her lips. "I can smell their stench all over you." She tipped her head back and slowly turned in a circle. "But I can sense something else in the air, tonight."

"What would that be?" Megan asked.

"Betrayal." Santé told her. She twirled around and growled at her niece. "You have brought them here, haven't you girl?"

"Who are you talking about?" Megan asked her aunt.

"Show me what I seek to find," Santé chanted as she waved her arms around the circle she stood in. The wind picked up and began to howl as the vegetation around them began bending to her will.

The ring on Jillian's finger began to glow and the wind died down. Channel snapped her head toward Jillian to stare at the ring.

"What magic is this?" Santé screamed. She turned to her niece and demanded, "Give me your locket so I can combine its power with mine." She held out her hand for the locket.

Megan reached out her hand and snatched her aunt's locket from her throat. "I don't think so, how about if I take yours instead?"

Santé growled and rushed her niece. Her hands were curled into claws and her eyes were filled with rage.

"Stop." Jillian called out. She came out of the tall grass and moved toward Santé and Megan.

Santé turned to look at her. "And who the hell are you? What do you want here?"

"I want you." Jillian told Santé. She reached into her pocket and brought out the jewel Destiny gave her. The jewel began to glow as did the stone in the two lockets in Megan's hands.

Santé turned her head and saw what was happening. She tried to snatch the lockets away from Megan but Jillian raised her hand. The ring on her finger began to glow and Santé couldn't move.

"What have you done to me, witch?" Santé screamed.

"I'm not a witch." Jillian told her. She looked at Megan and asked, "Will you bring the lockets to me?"

Megan nodded and stepped toward her.

"Don't give her the power of the lockets!" Santé screamed. She struggled to get free but the ring held her in place. "She will destroy our clan."

Megan didn't hesitate to hand over the lockets. Then she turned to glare at her aunt. "No Santé, she won't destroy us, you are the one that did that. You turned to the dark side a long time ago. You brought nothing but shame and despair to us."

Jillian held the two lockets and the jewel in her hand and the glow grew engulfing all three. When the glow began to throw off heat all three stones began to levitate into the air. They spun around faster and faster until the circle grew to hold two people. The woman Jillian and Seth knew as Destiny and Chantez Lamprey were in the circle.

Destiny held her hand out and the circling stone stopped in midair. She reached out and plucked the stones from the air. Looking at the stones in her hand she looked at Jillian. "Well done. I will take these stone back to where they belong." She turned to Chantez and nodded.

Chantez stepped out of the circle and went over to

Santé. "I believe you have something that belongs to me. I want my husband back."

Santé spit on her. "I will never give him back to you." She turned her head to see the rest of Chantez's family come out into the open, then she turned back to face Chantez. "I know you have the power to send me back to hell but I'll take him with me. You'll never see your husband again, not in this life or the next."

Megan walked up to her aunt and slapped her face. Santé turned her face toward her niece and glared at her. Megan then reached to her aunt's belt and snatched off a charm. She took a step back and Santé screamed at her."

"Don't you dare break that charm girl. I won't allow it."

Megan turned to her aunt. "There is a special hell for people like you and I hope you suffer greatly when she sends you there. You used all of us for your own gain. This ends here and now." Megan watched her aunt eyes as she snapped the charm in half and dropped the pieces of the charm to the ground.

The pieces began to glow and soon they shimmered. A moment later the shimmering grew and when it stopped a man's essence stood there. He was an older man with white hair brushed away from his face. He looked tired and weak but otherwise okay.

"Father." Channel whispered as she stumbled toward him. Benjamin and Jean also rushed up to him. They tried to hold him up but there was nothing solid to hold on to. Jean and Benjamin watched their mother move

185

closer to him. She held out her hand and laid it on his cheek.

"Oh Sebastian, what has she done to you?" Chantez whispered.

Sebastian smiled at his wife. "She knew the worst thing she could do to us was keep us apart." He glanced over to Santé. "She tore my soul from my body and trapped me in the charm. I had to watch helplessly as she fed my body to the gators."

Chantez closed her eyes. "I felt your pain that day. It was agonizing. I looked for your essence everywhere I could think of."

Sebastian pulled her into his arms. "Mon deuz, I have missed you wife."

"And for that she will pay." Chantez told him. She turned to where Santé was trapped. As she walked over to her Chantez began to chant. With each word she uttered the look of horror on Santé's face grew.

When the chant was finished Santé screamed and the shadows around her grew to pull her down into the ground. When she was finally gone Chantez turned to Jillian. "You have done everything I asked of you plus more. You gave me my husband back and for that I thank you from the bottom of my soul. Now I would ask one more thing."

Jillian waited for the words to come.

"Please give me my ring back." Chantez asked.

Jillian smiled. She reached for the ring on her hand and took it off. She handed it to Chantez, who in turn motioned for her granddaughter. "You should have gotten this from your own mother, but with Santé still around I couldn't take the chance it would fall into her hands."

"Oh Grandmere," Sarene whispered. "I'll take care of your legacy and pass it down to future generations. Thank you."

Chantez looked at her husband. "I think it's time to go now."

Sebastian smiled. "I think you're right." He hesitated then turned to Megan, "How did you know I was trapped in that charm?"

Megan smiled. "When I was a child my aunt used to let me play with her charms. One day your face appeared. I didn't know you were in there and you smiled at me. I never told my aunt about it, but I always remembered it. I was hoping you were still there."

Sebastian smiled. "Thank god, you remembered."

Chantez turned, and taking her husband's hand rejoined Destiny. Destiny smiled and tipping her head back the sand began to swirl around them and then they were gone.

"Wow." Seth whispered.

"How do we thank you for what you have done for our family?" Sarene asked Seth and Jillian.

"There is no need to thank us." Jillian told her. "We didn't do this for any type of reward."

"No, you did this because it needed to be done and you had the courage to do it." Jean said. "For that I thank you, but my niece is correct. How do we thank you?"

"Family is all we have when it comes right down to it. We have to protect them at any cost. I truly believe that." Jillian told them.

"And sometimes we all need a little help." Seth said.

"I think we should go home now." Channel said. "We've all been through a lot."

Jillian and Seth watched as the Lamprey's left the bayou. Eric had his arm around Megan's shoulders and Channel and Sarene followed Benjamin and Jean. The Lamprey family had gain and lost so much in the past few days, but at least they were whole again.

"I'm glad things worked out for them." Jillian said.

"Everything turned out okay here but what if it hadn't?" Seth asked.

"Do you finally believe in something you can't see or feel?"

Seth turned his head and looked at her. "I know. I didn't believe any of this when our adventure began, but I believe now. There are more things out there that I don't understand."

"Well, what should we do now?" Jillian asked.

"I have no idea." Seth told her. "Going back to my old life just doesn't seem so exciting right now."

"I know what you mean." Jillian told him. "I certainly never expected all of this when I bought the Inn. Who knew what secrets the Inn was hiding?"

"Who knows what secrets any old house holds?" Seth smiled mysteriously.